Ernest J. Gaines
A Gathering of Old Men

Ernest J. Gaines was born on a plantation in Pointe Coupée Parish near New Roads, Louisiana, which is the Bayonne of all his fictional works. His novels include the much-acclaimed *The Autobiography of Miss Jane Pittman, Of Love and Dust, Catherine Carmier, Bloodline,* and *In My Father's House.* He divides his time between San Francisco and the University of Southwestern Louisiana, in Lafayette, where he holds a visiting professorship in creative writing. His new novel, *A Lesson Before Dying,* will be published by Alfred A. Knopf in 1993.

Also by Ernest J. Gaines

Catherine Carmier

Of Love and Dust

Bloodline

The Autobiography of Miss Jane Pittman

A Long Day in November

In My Father's House

A Gathering of Old Men

Ernest J. Gaines

Vintage Contemporaries

Vintage Books · A Division of Random House, Inc. · New York

FIRST VINTAGE CONTEMPORARIES EDITION, JULY 1992

Copyright © 1983 by Ernest J. Gaines

All rights reserved under International and Pan-American Copyright
Conventions. Published in the United States by Vintage Books,
a division of Random House, Inc., New York, and simultaneously
in Canada by Random House of Canada Limited, Toronto.
Originally published by Alfred A. Knopf, Inc. in 1983.

Portions of this book have appeared previously in
Black Scholar and *Georgia Review*.

Library of Congress Cataloging in Publications Data
Gaines, Ernest J., 1933–
A gathering of old men.
I. Title
[PS3557.A355G3   1984b]   813´.54   91-58064
ISBN 0-679-73890-8

Manufactured in the United States of America
13579E8642

This book is dedicated to the memory of
Mr. Walter Zeno—aka Salute, Rider, Pete,
and a few other names

A Gathering of Old Men

George Eliot, Jr.

aka

Snookum

I heard Candy out in the front yard calling Gram Mon. Me and Toddy and Minnie was sitting at the table eating, and Gram Mon was at the stove looking in the pot to see if she had enough food left in there for supper. I could hear Candy out in the yard, going: "Oh, Aunt Glo; oh, Aunt Glo; oh, Aunt Glo." I jumped up from my chair to go see what she wanted, but Gram Mon told me to sit back down there and finish my food, 'cause my name wasn't Glo, or Aunt. She looked at me long enough for it to set in; then she started toward the front door where Candy was still going: "Oh, Aunt Glo; oh, Aunt Glo; oh, Aunt Glo."

Old Toddy with his snagged-teef self looked at me and grinned, 'cause he thought Gram Mon had hurt my feeling when she told me to sit back down. I checked one of my fist, but he knowed I couldn't hit him, 'cause he had already caught me and Minnie playing mama and papa in the weeds, and he told me I had a year when I couldn't do him nothing no matter what he did me, and if I did he was go'n tell Gram Mon what he caught us doing. He told me he could grin at me all he wanted to, and he could hit me, and kick me, and pinch me (in church, or home, he didn't care), and he could steal my cake if he wanted to, or my candy if I had any, and he could lose all his marbles to me, and I better not take them back, and I better not gig his spinning top when we played gigging, 'cause if I did he was go'n tell Gram Mon what he saw me and Minnie trying to do in the weeds. He said it was go'n be like that a whole year, if I liked it or not. It started just 'fore Candy started calling Gram Mon, 'cause we had just come in to eat dinner when I heard her calling out there in the yard.

I heard Candy saying: "Snookum in there?"

"At the table eating. What's the matter, Candy?" Gram Mon said.

"Get Snookum out here," Candy said.

"Snookum did something wrong?" Gram Mon asked her.

"Hurry, Aunt Glo," Candy said.

"Snookum?" Gram Mon called me.

Old Toddy and Minnie jumped up too, and Gram Mon looked over her shoulder and said, "Get back in there and eat them turnips. I called Snookum."

"How come Snookum don't have to eat his turnips?" Toddy said. "How come just me and Minnie got to eat turnips?"

" 'Cause I called him," Gram Mon said. "Now, get back in there and finish them turnips."

"I ain't no turnip-eating machine," Toddy said.

"You better turn into one 'fore I get back in that kitchen," Gram Mon said. "Snookum, Candy want talk to you. Toddy, you and Minnie finish them turnips," Gram Mon said.

"Snookum can act a fool and laugh at me out there," Toddy said. "But he know I got something on him."

Candy was standing in the yard close to the steps when I came out on the garry. She wore a white shirt and khaki pants and brown shoes with little gold buckles. Her hair was light brown and dark brown and cut short, almost short like a man's hair.

"Come here, Snookum," she said.

I jumped down on the ground where she was, and she grabbed me by the shoulders with both hands. She leaned over and brought her face close to mine, and her eyes, the color of blue smoke, looked wild and scared. I was thinking I had done something wrong and she was mad at me for it.

"Now, listen," she said. "I want you to run, and I don't want you to stop running. I want you to go tell Rufe and Reverend Jameson and Corrine and the rest of them to gather at Mathu's house right away. And I want you to go to the front, and I want you to—listen to me good, now," she said, squeezing my shoulders and hurting me a little bit—"go up to the house and see if Miss Merle's there. If she is, tell her I say come quick. No, if she's there tell her to call Lou and tell Lou to get here quick, then she get here quick. If she's not there, tell Janey to call her and Lou and tell them to get here quick. Don't waste time on that phone talking, just get here quick. Don't do nothing but get here quick. You heard what I said, Snookum?"

"What I'm telling all them people to get here quick for?" I asked her.

"That's none of your business, Snookum. You're nothing but a little boy. Now, get moving and don't stop running."

I shot out of the yard. When I hit the road, I saw the tractor in front of Mathu's house. The motor was running, I could hear it, I could see the smoke, but Charlie wasn't on the tractor. He had two big loads of cane hitched to the back of the tractor, but he wasn't on the tractor. On the other side of the road, in front of Mathu's house, I could see Candy's big black car shining in the sun. I knowed Candy didn't tell me to tell Mathu anything, but looked to me like since all them other people was gathering at his house, looked to me like he ought to know what was going on, too. So when I came up even with his house, I ran in the yard, and that's when I seen Beau. Beau was laying over there in the weeds all bloody.

"Get away from there, boy!" Mathu hollered at me from the garry.

"I'm doing something for Candy," I said.

"You ain't doing nothing for her there," he said. "Now, get away from there."

Mathu was squatting against the wall with that double-barrel shotgun in his arms. He had on that old gray hat that was the color of the ground. He had on a dirty white tee shirt and green pants. He was smoking a cigarette. Mathu was black black with a white beard.

"Candy want everybody at your house," I told him.

"If that's what she want, you better go on and do it," he said. "Now, get away from there."

I looked back at that tractor. The motor was still running. I looked back at Mathu squatting against the wall.

"Where Charlie?" I said. "How come he ain't driving that tractor?"

"That's none of your business," Mathu said. "Get out of this yard, and get out fast, or I'll come out there and tear your butt with a switch."

Mathu started getting up, and I shot out of there, headed up the quarters, spanking my butt the way you spank your horse when you want him to run fast. Rufe was hoeing in the garden when I got to his house. The garden was behind the house, and you could always hear Rufe back there working and singing. When I told him what Candy had said, he looked at me a second like he was trying to figure out what Candy wanted him for; then all of a sudden he threw the hoe down and started running. I yanked my horse around and shot out too, headed up the quarters. I figured this time of day Corrine was in her kitchen eating, so I didn't bother to knock on the front door. I just ran through the house back in the kitchen. She was sitting at the table eating greens and rice out of a pan. Eating all by herself. She didn't have no children or a husband. She was just by herself—eating and looking out of the back door. When I told her what Candy had said, she turned slowly to look at me, and her eyes was all brownish and tired-looking. She didn't say a thing. Didn't say "Uh-huh" or nothing. Just looked old and tired-looking. Eating on her front teef—looking old and tired-looking. I turned around and shot out of there, spanking my butt the way you spank a horse when you want that horse to run fast. Reverend Jameson had just come out of the house when I ran in his yard. Me and Reverend Jameson didn't get along too good. He was always getting on me, saying I should be in the church serving the Lord instead of shooting marbles and playing ball. I told him what Candy had said, and he looked down the quarters, but he couldn't see a thing from here for all the weeds. 'Fore he could ask me anything, I had already turned and was headed up the quarters. I wasn't going in the people's yards anymore, I was just hollering to the people from out in the road. I didn't see half of the people I was hollering at. I didn't even know if they was home. You had too much weeds and bushes even to see the houses sometime. I just hollered names; running, spanking my butt, and hollering names. "Candy want y'all at Mathu's house! Candy want y'all at Mathu's house! Candy want y'all at Mathu's house!"

When I came up to Marshall House, I was tired and I could just barely make it across the pasture up to the flower garden. I didn't go in, I called Janey from the gate. Just calling and calling her. Took her a long time to come out on the garry, and she came out there fussing.

"What's the matter with you, boy?" she said to me. "Don't you know the Major and Miss Bea in there trying to sleep?"

"Candy sent me," I said.

"She didn't tell you to wake up the dead, did she?"

Janey looked at me a good while 'fore she came down the steps. She had on a white dress and white shoes and an apron. She was heavy as Gram Mon, but not old as Gram Mon, and not light as Gram Mon. While she took her own good time coming to the gate, I looked at a couple of butterflies flitting around the flowers in the corner of the yard. Home, the butterflies wouldn'ta had a chance. But I knowed Janey woulda killed me if she even thought I was thinking 'bout coming in that yard.

"What's the matter with you?" she said, at the gate.

"Candy want you to call Lou," I said.

"You say 'Mr. Lou,' and you say 'Miss Candy,'" Janey said, looking down at me from the other side of the gate. "I don't care how libbel they is, you still a child. You say Mister and Miss round me. You ain't too old for me to tan your butt, you know."

"Miss Merle in there?" I asked her.

"No, she ain't," Janey said.

"Guess you'll have to do then," I said.

"Thank you, sir," Janey said, looking over the gate at me. "I 'preciates that."

"Call Lou," I said. "Tell him Candy want him here right away. And call Miss Merle."

"And what I just told you no more than a minute ago about saying Mister and Miss round me?"

She looked at me hard a long time. That's how they do when they want you to remember something.

"What Candy want with them down in the quarters?" she asked me.

"Something to do with Mathu and Beau. Beau laying on his back in Mathu's yard. And Mathu squatting there with that shotgun."

Janey's face changed quick. She was mad at first, now she

was scared. She pushed that gate open and grabbed me in the collar.

"That shot I heard?" she said. "That shot I heard?"

"That hurt," I said, jerking away from her. "Y'all got any tea cakes or plarines in there?"

"Boy," Janey said, and raised her hand to hit me. She wasn't mad, she was scared. I ducked out of her way.

"That's what I heard?" she asked again. Now she looked like she wanted to cry. "That's the shot I heard?"

"I guess so, I don't know," I said.

Now she started whooping. "Lord, have mercy. Lord, Jesus, have mercy. Boy, you know what this mean? Mean Fix coming here with his drove. You too young to know Fix. But I know Fix."

She started back to the house. I looked at her through the gate.

"You getting me some tea cakes?" I called to her. "Candy didn't pay me nothing to come up here."

She didn't answer me. Just kept on walking. Now she was wiping her eyes with her apron.

"Hanh?" I called to her. I had my face right up against the gate. "You getting me some tea cakes, or a plarine?"

She went back in the house. Paid me no more 'tention than she did them butterflies around that flower. I left the gate and went on back down the quarters. I didn't get a nickel or a tea cake or a plarine for running all the way up there. But I still had one thing on old Toddy. He didn't see what I saw.

Janice Robinson

aka

Janey

L o r d have mercy, Jesus, what now? Where do I turn? Go where first? The Major? For what? He's already drunk out there on that front garry, and it's just twelve o'clock. Miss Bea? That's like talking to the wall. Where? Mr. Lou? Yes. She said call Mr. Lou. Mr. Lou and Miss Merle. I better make it Mr. Lou first. Lord, have mercy, keep me on my feet if it is thy holy will.

I went in and dialed the paper in Baton Rouge—my finger trembling, just a-trembling. When the operator answered, I told her I wanted to speak to Mr. Lou Dimes. She told me that was "City," and told me to hold on. Then somebody else answered and said, "City"; then he said, "Toby Wright." I told him I wanted to speak to Mr. Lou Dimes. "Lou at dinner right now," he said. "Oh, Lord," I said. "Where? Find him. Hurry. Candy want him here right away. Please, sir. Please." "Just hold on," he said. "Calm down. He'll be back in a little while. Who am I speaking to? That's you, Janey?" "Yes, sir, it's me," I said. "Find him fast as you can, and tell him get here fast as he can. He don't have to call. Just get here. And please hurry. Hurry."

I was crying so hard when I got through talking to him I had to wipe my whole face with my apron. Then I dialed Miss Merle. But nobody answered. I let it ring a dozen times, but no answer. Lord, Jesus, I told myself. Lord, Jesus, help me.

I went out on the front garry. The Major was all curled up in the swing, sleeping. His face resting on the back of his hands. A half glass of watered whiskey on the banister by the swing. Lord, Jesus, I thought to myself, it ain't evening yet, and he's already drunk. Lord, Jesus, help me. I went back inside and started upstairs to Miss Bea's room, but halfway up I remembered she wasn't in her room, she was out in the back pasture. I went to the back door and looked—and there she was, way over yonder, under one of them pecan trees, a little bitty thing, ain't five foot tall, feeling in all them weeds with a stick for pecans. Lord, Jesus, I thought to myself, now just s'posing, just s'posing, now, a snake or something come up there and bite that old woman in all them weeds. Lord, Jesus, I said, help me. Help me if it is thy holy will, Lord, Jesus.

I went back and dialed Miss Merle's number again, but she still wasn't there. Help me, Lord, Jesus, I said. Please help this your humbled servant who ain't never done nothing but served thee well. I went back and looked at the Major—still curled up there sleeping, snoring now. I got the glass of watered whiskey and took it back in the kitchen, and while I was there I looked across the pasture at that old woman out in them weeds looking for pecans with a stick. See? I thought. See? If anything bite that old woman, they'll blame me. Lord, Jesus, I said, help me, Lord, Jesus. Help me. I went back and dialed Miss Merle again, but she still wasn't there. Lord, Jesus, I said, help me, Lord, Jesus. I went out on the wes' garry and looked down the quarters, but you couldn't see a thing down there for all the weeds. Lord, Jesus, I said to myself, help me, Lord, Jesus. I looked toward the highway, toward the river, 'cause I expected to hear Fix and his drove coming in them trucks with them guns any minute now. Lord, Jesus, I said to myself, help me, Lord, Jesus. I went back in and dialed Miss Merle again, but she still wasn't home. Lord, Jesus, I said, help me, Lord, Jesus.

I started my dusting again, 'cause that's what I was doing 'fore that boy come up there making all that racket. I hadn't picked up the mop more than ten minutes when I heard the car drive up in the front yard. I ran out on the front garry and seen it was Miss Merle, and looked like a heavy load just fell off my shoulders. I ran down the steps to meet her in the yard.

She was smiling. Always smiling. Just a good-natured person. The nicest I have ever known.

"Lord, have mercy, I'm so glad you got here," I said.

She seen I had been crying, and she stopped smiling.

"What's the matter?" she said.

She was a fat lady with a nice round face and she had a little pointed nose and a little red mouth and gray eyes. She looked like a owl more than anything else, and that's what the people in the quarters called her behind her back—Miss Owl.

"Something the matter?" she asked again. She looked at the Major all curled up in the swing. "Jack drunk," she said. She looked at the gold watch on her short, fat arm. "Not even twelve-thirty yet," she said.

"I been calling and calling your house," I told her.

"I was on my way over here," she said. "What's the matter? What happened?"

"Candy," I said.

"What about Candy?"

"They been a killing," I said.

"What?" she said. Her gray eyes looked hard at me, but behind all that hardness I could see she was scared. "Candy?" she said.

"No'm. Beau," I said.

"Beau?" she said. "Candy? Beau? What happened?"

"Beau dead," I said.

"Candy?" she said.

"I don't know," I said.

"Where's Candy?"

"In the quarters," I said.

"What's she doing down there?"

"That's where it happened," I said. "Mathu's house."

"Oh, my God, my God," she said, and throwed her hand up to her mouth. She looked toward the garry where the Major was curled up in the swing sleeping. "Jack?" she called to him. "Jack? Jack?"

"He can't hear you," I said.

"Where's Bea?" Miss Merle asked me.

"In the back yard looking for pecans," I said. "Miss Merle, Candy want you down the quarters right away."

"Who else know about this?" Miss Merle asked.

"Just the people in the quarters," I said. "She wanted me to notify you and Mr. Lou, but nobody else."

"You got Lou?" she asked me.

"He's at dinner," I told her.

"Oh, shit," she said, and looked toward the garry again. "Jack? Jack?" she called.

"He don't hear you," I said. "He's been like that since 'leven o'clock."

"I better get down there," Miss Merle said.

She got back in the car. She was so fat she had a hard time doing it.

"Pray," she said. "Pray, Janey."

I knowed she was talking about Fix and his drove.

"Pray, Janey," she said, swinging that car around. She was backing over flowers, over little bushes, little trees, spraying gravel all over the place, all over me, too. "Pray," she said, going out the yard. "Pray."

I went back in the house. She didn't have to tell me to pray. I was doing that long 'fore she got there.

Myrtle Bouchard

aka

Miss Merle

I had Lucy bake me an apple pie, because I knew how much Jack just liked his apple pie. I told Lucy when she came to work that morning if she baked me the best apple pie she ever baked in her life I would give her half the day off. She told me don't worry. And I'll be darn if she didn't bake the best one I had ever seen or tasted. Golden brown and sweet, but not too sweet—just sweet enough. I told her, at twelve o'clock sharp, she could take off because I am a woman of my word. She said, "Don't I already know that, Miss Merle?" Bless her heart. She said, "Why you think I baked the best apple pie I ever baked in my life? And the next one go'n be twice as good."

We both left the house at the same time, she going to her place at Medlow, and I on my way to Marshall to see Jack and Bea. The pie was for Jack—and, Lord, I wished he liked me much as he did apple pie. But I had been saying that for years and years now.

When I drove into the yard, I saw Janey coming out of the house in a hurry. I knew something was wrong, and when she came out into the yard I could see that she had been crying.

Then she told me. And I thought to myself, My Lord, my Lord. I looked at Jack asleep there in the swing, and I thought to myself, My Lord, my Lord.

I forgot all about the apple pie. I hurried back into the car and sped out of the yard. Turning down into the quarters, I could see the tractor in the middle of the road, and I could see Candy's black LTD parked in the ditch on the right. But I didn't see any of the people as I drove past the old houses. Just like little bedbugs, I told myself. Just like frightened little bedbugs now. But when I stopped before Mathu's house, I could see they were not bedbugs after all. They were all there, in the yard, and on the porch. Three of them had shotguns— Mathu, Johnny Paul, and Rufe. None of the women had guns; they and the children just sat there watching me. Candy was in the road by the time I got out of the car.

"I killed Beau," she said.

I was still looking past her at Mathu and Rufe and Johnny Paul with those old shotguns. Mathu squatted against the wall by the door, the gun cradled in his arms. Squatting, not sitting or standing, was his favorite position when he was out on the porch. And by the door, against the wall, was his favorite place to be. Johnny Paul sat on the steps with his gun, and Rufe leaned back against the end of the porch with his. I had never seen anything like this in all my life before, and I wasn't too sure I was seeing it now.

"What?" I said, still watching the porch.

"I shot Beau," Candy said.

I looked back at her. I didn't jerk my head around, I looked at her slowly. I had known Candy over twenty-five years. She was no more than five or six when her mother and father were killed in a car wreck, and I had helped raise her. Surely, Mathu here in the quarters, and I at the main house had done as much to raise her as had her uncle and aunt. Maybe even more than they. Yes, he and I had done more than they. So I knew when she was lying to me, and I knew she was lying to me now.

"Candy, what's going on down here?" I asked her.

"Listen," she said. She was small, not more than five two, and thin as a dime. She wore the wrong clothes, and that hair was cropped too short for a young woman interested in catching a man. But Candy was not. A young man came around, but I had no idea what kind of relationship they had. Probably the same kind Jack and I had. "I don't know what's going on," she said. "I wanted you or Lou here before Mapes got here. I don't—"

"What are they doing with those guns?" I asked her.

"I don't know, Miss Merle," she said. "I shot him. But all of a sudden Mathu said he shot him. Then all of a sudden Rufe said he shot him. Johnny Paul was nowhere around here. But after he came here and saw what had happened, he said he had as much reason to shoot Beau as anybody, so he ran home and got his old gun. But I shot him."

I looked at him lying over there in the weeds. The weeds were so high I could hardly see anything more than just the tip of his cowboy boots. And I sure wasn't going any closer to get a better look at the rest of him.

"Don't they know who that is?" I said to Candy.

"They know," she said. "They just want the credit for shooting him. But I shot him."

"Here in Mathu's yard, Candy? Mapes is no fool, you know."

"I shot him," she said. "You got to believe me. I don't care if Mapes does or not. I need you to believe me. Clinton can handle Mapes in court."

"And who's going to handle Fix, Candy?" I asked her. "Before you even get to court? Fix?"

"I shot him," she said. "You must believe that."

"No," I said.

"Yes," she said.

"No," I said, shaking my head. I looked past her at Mathu squatting against that wall with that gun cradled in his arms. He was smoking a cigarette now. He knew I was looking at him, but he was looking past me at the tractor out there in the road. The rest of the people watched quietly from the porch and the steps.

"I won't let them touch my people," she said. "I did it."

I looked back at her. She knew that I had been looking at him.

"That's how it's going to be," she said. She knew that I knew better, though.

"Candy?" I said.

"Now, I want you to do something for me," she said quickly.

"The best thing I can do for you is make you tell me the truth, Candy," I said.

"I told you the truth," she said. But she knew that I knew better. "Now, you can do one of two things," she said. "Help me or leave."

"Leave?" I said. I didn't have to look at Beau again. I didn't have to look at Mathu. She knew I wouldn't leave, couldn't leave. "Leave?" I said.

"Help me, then," she said.

"Help you how, Candy?"

"I need more guns," she said.

"What?"

"Get me more twelve-gauge shotguns," she said. "Get me more people here."

"More people?" I asked her. "More people for what, Candy?"

"You see what they're doing?" she said, nodding toward the porch.

I had already seen them, so I didn't have to look again. "I see old men with shotguns, I see that," I said.

"Yes," she said. "And I need more. Mapes come here, he'll beat up two till they talk, then he'll take one. I need more people here."

"Candy, are you crazy?" I said. "Are you crazy? Do you know what you're saying?"

"I know what I'm saying, I know what I'm doing," she said. "Get me some more people here quick."

"Get who?" I said.

"Who?" she said. She looked at me the way you look at somebody playing dumb. But I was not playing dumb; I didn't know who she was talking about. "Who?" she said again. "There's not a black family in this parish Fix and his crowd hasn't hurt sometime or other. You're older than I am, you know that better than I do. Get any of them, get all of them. Now is their chance to stand."

"And be killed? Is that what you want? Blood all over this place?"

"Look around you, Miss Merle," she said, waving her hand toward the porch. I didn't have to look around to know how quietly they sat, watching and listening. "Aren't they ready to die?" she asked. "Look at Mathu. Do you know who Mathu is, Miss Merle? Miss Merle, I ask, do you know who Mathu is?"

"I know who Mathu is, Candy," I told her. "I knew Mathu long before you were ever born."

And I looked at her long enough to let her know that I knew it was he who had done it, and not she. She turned away quickly.

"Look at Rufe," she said, trying to throw my mind off Mathu. "Look at Johnny Paul."

"Candy?" I said.

"We don't have much time," she said. "We have to notify Mapes sooner or later. I want an hour jump on him at least. I want Lou here before he gets here. I want more people here with twelve-gauge shotguns, and number five shells. Empty number five shells. Empty. Now, you don't have much time. Talk to Janey."

"Talk to Janey about what, Candy?"

"In case you have forgotten what Fix has done to these people around here, maybe she can remind you. I will not let Mapes or Fix harm my people."

"Candy?" I said. I reached out to take her arm, but she moved back out of my reach. "Candy?" I said.

"No, I won't let them harm my people," she said. "I will protect my people. My daddy and all them before him did, and I—"

"Candy?" I said.

"I'll stand alone," she said. "Before I let them harm my people, I'll stand alone."

"Candy, please. Please, Candy," I said.

"I did it," she said.

"Nobody in this parish will ever believe that."

"I don't care what people in this parish believe," she said. "What do I care about what people in this parish believe? I'll stand alone."

I turned from her and looked at Mathu squatting there, black as pitch, with that double-barrel shotgun cradled in his arms. How many times had I stood in that yard talking to him while he squatted there, and she sitting across from him at the end of the porch? How many times had I driven by, not stopping, but waving at him while he squatted there, and she sitting on the steps or at the end of the porch talking to him? How many times had I sat on the porch at Marshall House talking to him while he sat on the steps, holding his hat between his knees, and she sitting on the banister closer to him than she was to me, her aunt, or her uncle? How many times? How many times? How many times?

I turned back to her. But before I could open my mouth, she was already saying it again. "I did it."

"What I ought to do is get away from here," I told her. "That's what I should've done years ago. But I don't have any sense. I never had any sense. Have I?"

"You and Lou are all that I have to turn to," she said.

"Sure," I said. "Two of a kind. Both fools. We both should've gone other directions years ago. But no, no."

"Go talk to Janey," she said.

"I didn't say anything about going along—"

"Make her give you some names," she said. She had not heard one word that I had said. "Lot of names," she said. "Twelve-gauge shotguns and number five shells. Empty number five shells. When Mapes gets here, I'm going to need a lot of empty number five shells."

"Sure," I said. "Because that's the size he used on Beau."

That quieted her for a second, but only a second. Then she was right back again.

"Put Janey out on the west gallery to look out for Lou. When Lou passes by the house, call Mapes. Don't call Mapes till Lou passes by. I want Lou here first. If you ever loved this family, if you ever loved me. Please."

"I hope I didn't," I said, looking at her. "I hope I had never heard of any of you."

I looked across the toes of those cowboy boots at Mathu squatting there with that shotgun. He had lit another cigarette. He wasn't even looking toward us anymore. He was looking down the quarters. Toward what? There was nothing to see from here but the tall bloodweeds that grew on the ditch bank and beside the road. I turned away without saying another word.

It took me two or three minutes to get back to Marshall House. I started blowing the horn before I came into the yard, and by the time I stopped the car Janey was already out there. Jack was still asleep in the swing.

"Get that apple pie off the back seat and follow me," I told her. "Where's Bea?"

"The wes' garry," Janey said.

"Jack?" I said, going up the steps. "Jack?"

"He can't hear you," Janey said.

I went over to the swing and shook him. "Jack? Jack?"

"It's no use," Janey said.

"Jack?" I called, shaking him again. He didn't even grunt. "Oh, the hell with him. He never wanted any part of it anyhow."

Janey and I went inside. While she took the pie to the kitchen, I went out to the west gallery looking for Bea. I found her sitting in her rocking chair by the door, gazing across the flower garden toward the trees in the outer pasture. Beyond the trees was the road that led you down into the quarters. At the mouth of the road was the main highway, heading toward Bayonne, and just on the other side of the highway was the St. Charles River. A light breeze had just risen up from the river, and I caught a faint odor from the sweet-olive bush which stood in the far right corner of the garden.

"Bea, I have to talk to you," I said.

"That's you, Merle?" she said, looking over her shoulder at me. "Good. Now I can have my pea picker. It's almost one o'clock. Where's Janey? Oh, Janey?" she called.

"Bea," I said, standing in front of her. "We don't have time for pea pickers, Bea."

"Nonsense," she said. "When didn't you have time for a pea picker? Where is Janey?"

"Bea," I said. "Don't you know what's happened?"

"I don't care what's happened," she said. She looked back toward the screen door. "Janey?" she called.

"Yes, Ma'am?" Janey said, coming outside.

"You know what time it is?" Bea asked, looking up at her.

Janey looked at me. She didn't know what to do.

"Bea," I said. "A man is dead. A man is dead in the quarters, Bea. Beau Boutan is dead."

"Well?" she said. "What can I do about it? People die all the time. I'm going to die, you're going to die. Janey, you know what time it is?"

"Don't move, Janey," I said. "I need you out here, Bea," I said. "Did you hear me? A man is dead. Beau Boutan was shot down in the quarters. And Candy is down there claiming she did it. Do you understand what I'm trying to say to you?"

"That gal got spunk," Bea said. "Always said she had spunk. That's why she won't get married, all that spunk. Janey, go in there and get those pea pickers."

"Don't you move, Janey," I said.

"What did you say?" Bea asked, looking up at me. Her little overpowdered white face was as wrinkled as a prune. Her blue-dyed hair was so thin you could see her gray skull. Only her grayish-blue eyes were still alive and youthful, but now angry. "What did you say?" she asked me again. "You told her 'don't'? This is not Seven Oaks, Miss, this is Marshall. At Marshall I say 'don't' and I say 'do.'" She looked at Janey just as hard as she had looked at me. "What are you waiting on?" she asked her.

"Yes, Ma'am," Janey said, and went back inside.

She must have had the drinks already mixed and sitting in the refrigerator, because she was back with two of them within a couple of minutes. The drink was made of gin and pink lemonade, garnished with a slice of orange, a cherry, a piece of lime, a sprig of mint, and a paper straw the color of a peppermint stick. I set my drink on the banister, but Bea couldn't wait to get started on hers. It was her first drink of the day, and she was already running more than a half hour late. Janey and I stood there watching her.

"Now, what did you say Candy did?" she asked. "That gal got spunk. Just like Grandpa Nate."

"My God," I said. "My God, Beatrice. Candy just told me she killed somebody. Is that all you got to say, she's just like her grandpa?"

"My grandpa," she said. "Her great-great grandpa. Her grandpa grandpa. About time she shot one of them Cajuns, messing up the land with those tractors. Yes, that gal's got spunk in her."

I could see that I was wasting my time talking to Beatrice, and I turned to Janey. Janey was standing there looking down at her and biting her lips as if she were about to start crying again.

"Hold up, Janey," I told her. "I need somebody around here with me. Now you hold up now."

"I'm strong," she said.

"You better be strong," I said. "Now, listen. I want nothing but answers. Nothing but answers. No questions. Answers. Who do you know don't like Fix?"

"Ma'am?" she said, drawing back and looking at me as though I were out of my mind. You would have thought I had just asked her who did she know who liked the devil.

"I told you no questions, Janey, just answers," I said. "We don't have time for both of us to ask questions. I ask the questions, you answer them. Now, who do you know don't like Fix?"

"I don't like him," Bea said. "I've never liked him. Why we ever let that kind on this land, I don't know. The land has not been the same since they brought those tractors here."

"Beatrice, please shut up," I said. "Please. Please, Beatrice." She raised the glass and sucked on the straw again. "Janey, who do you know don't like Fix?"

"I don't know nobody do like Fix," she said.

"Do you think they hate him enough to stand up to Mapes?"

"Ma'am?" she said.

"Janey, I warned you," I said. "Yes, or no. Will they stand, or won't they stand up to Mapes with empty shotguns?"

"I don't know what you talking about, Miss Merle," she said. She wanted to cry. "Please, Ma'am, I don't know what you talking about."

"I'll tell you what I'm talking about," I told her. "I'll tell you once, and I want answers from then on. You got a crazy thirty-year-old white gal down in the quarters claiming she just killed a white man. Now, I know she didn't—and Mathu did. But she's going to protect Mathu. She's going to protect him even if she has to get every other black person in this state involved. She's already got two old fools down there, Rufe and Johnny Paul, claiming they did it. But that's not enough for her. She wants more. Ten, fifteen, twenty, a thousand more. She wants them to get twelve-gauge shotguns, number five shells, fire the guns, keep the empty shells, so that when Mapes points his finger at Mathu, they can all say— Who do you know don't like Fix? Get them on that phone."

Now she started crying, bawling there like a lunatic. "Oh, Lord, have mercy, Jesus. Don't make me do nothing like that. Please, Miss Merle. Please, Ma'am, Miss Merle, don't make me do nothing like that."

I grabbed her in the collar and slapped her two or three times.

"Don't you tell me don't make you do nothing like that," I told her. "You think I'm having fun? You tell me who don't like Fix or I start slapping some more. Now, who don't like Fix?"

She threw her head back, her black, round face quivering there like jelly, and the tears just pouring down her cheeks. I knew I was being unmerciful, taking out my frustration on her, but I didn't care. If I was going to be in it, then they all would be in it. And if I had to slap her around to let her know she was going to be in it, then that was just too bad. "Who don't like Fix?" I asked her again.

"Clatoo, that's for sure," Bea said. "Bad blood been there for years."

I looked down at Bea, but she was already sucking on that straw again.

I tried to remember what Fix had done to Clatoo. I knew most of the history of that river and of that parish the past fifty years. I tried to remember now what Fix and Clatoo had had it about. Then I remembered. It was not Fix, it was that crazy brother of his, Forest Boutan, who had tried to rape one of Clatoo's sisters. She had defended herself by chopping him half dozen times with a cane knife. She didn't kill him, but he was well marked for the rest of his days. And she was sent to the pen for the rest of hers, where after so many years she died insane. That happened just before the Second World War.

"Clatoo still at Glenn?" I asked Janey.

She was still trying to get away from me, but I was known to have two of the strongest hands in St. Raphael Parish.

"Yes, Ma'am," she said when she couldn't break loose. "Still there, gardening."

"Has he got a phone?"

"I, I, I—" she said.

I yanked on the collar of her dress. "Speak up, dammit."

"He stay there with Emma," she said, crying.

"What name Emma goes under?"

"Henderson," she said. "I believe—yes, Ma'am. It's Henderson."

I turned her loose, and she started rubbing the side of her neck.

"I'm going in there and get that number out the phone book," I told her. "You and Bea think up some more names. Think up a dozen of them. We might as well all go to jail—

or all go to the crazy house—one. Where's that phone book?"

"On the table by the fireplace," Janey said.

"When I get through with Clatoo, you all better have me some more names ready," I said. "You hear me, don't you?"

"Yes, Ma'am," she said.

"First, get me another drink," Bea said, handing Janey the glass.

"Lord, have mercy," Janey said. "Don't I have enough trouble already, Miss Bea?"

"You take this glass and get in there and get me another drink," Bea said. "I'll help you with your names when you come back."

Janey took the glass, and I got my drink off the banister, and we went inside together. She went into the back to get Bea another drink, and I went to the phone to call Clatoo.

Robert Louis
Stevenson Banks

aka

Chimley

Me and Mat was down there fishing. We goes fishing every Tuesday and every Thursday. We got just one little spot now. Ain't like it used to be when you had the whole river to fish on. The white people, they done bought up the river now, and you got nowhere to go but that one little spot. Me and Mat goes there every Tuesday and Thursday. Other people uses it other days, but on Tuesday and Thursday they leaves it for us. We been going to that one little spot like that every Tuesday and Thursday the last ten, 'leven years. That one little spot. Just ain't got nowhere else to go no more.

We had been down there—oh, 'bout a hour. Mat had caught eight or nine good-size perches, and me about six—throw in a couple of sackalays there with the bunch. Me and Mat was just sitting there taking life easy, talking low. Mat was sitting on his croker sack, I was sitting on my bucket. The fishes we had caught, we had them on a string in the water, keeping them fresh. We was just sitting there talking low, talking 'bout the old days.

Then that oldest boy of Berto, that sissy one they called Fue, come running down the riverbank and said Clatoo said Miss Merle said that young woman at Marshall, Candy, wanted us on the place right away. She wanted us to get twelve-gauge shotguns and number five shells and she wanted us to shoot, but keep the empty shells and get there right away.

Me and Mat looked at him standing there sweating—a great big old round-face, sissy-looking boy, in blue jeans and a blue gingham shirt, the shirt wet from him running.

Mat said, "All that for what?"

The boy looked like he was ready to run some more. Sweat just pouring down the side of his face. He was one of them great big old sissy-looking boys—round, smooth, sissy-looking face.

He said: "Something to do with Mathu, and something to do with Beau Boutan dead in his yard. That's all I know, all I want to know. Up to y'all now, I done done my part. Y'all can go and do like she say or y'all can go home, lock y'all doors, and crawl under the bed like y'all used to. Me, I'm leaving."

He turned.

"Where you going?" Mat called to him.

"You and no Boutan'll ever know," he called back.

"You better run out of Louisiana," Mat said to himself.

The boy had already got out of hearing reach—one of them great big old sissy boys, running hard as he could go up the riverbank.

Me and Mat didn't look at each other for a while. Pretending we was more interested in the fishing lines. But it wasn't fishing we was thinking about now. We was thinking about what happened to us after something like this did happen. Not a killing like this. I had never knowed in all my life where a black man had killed a white man in this parish. I had knowed about fights, about threats, but not killings. And now I was thinking about what happened after these fights, these threats, how the white folks rode. This what I was thinking, and I was sure Mat was doing the same. That's why we didn't look at each other for a while. We didn't want to see what the other one was thinking. We didn't want to see the fear in the other one's face.

"He works in mysterious ways, don't He?" Mat said. It wasn't loud, more like he was talking to himself, not to me. But I knowed he was talking to me. He didn't look at me when he said it, but I knowed he was talking to me. I went on looking at my line.

"That's what they say," I said.

Mat went on looking at his line awhile. I didn't have to look and see if he was looking at his line. We had been together so much, me and him, I knowed what he was doing without looking at him.

"You don't have to answer this 'less you want to, Chimley," he said. He didn't say that loud, neither. He had just jerked on the line, 'cause I could hear the line cut through the water.

"Yeah, Mat?" I said.

He jerked on the line again. Maybe it was a turtle trying to get at the bait. Maybe he just jerked on the line to do something 'stead of looking at me.

"Scared?" he asked. His voice was still low. And he still wasn't looking at me.

"Yes," I said.

He jerked on the line again. Then he pulled in a sackalay 'bout long and wide as my hand. He rebaited the hook and spit on the bait for luck and throwed the line back out in the water. He didn't look at me all this time. I didn't look at him, either. Just seen all this out the corner of my eyes.

"I'm seventy-one, Chimley," he said after the line had settled again. "Seventy-one and a half. I ain't got too much strength left to go crawling under that bed like Fue said."

"I'm seventy-two," I said. But I didn't look at him when I said it.

We sat there awhile looking out at the lines. The water was so clean and blue, peaceful and calm. I coulda sat there all day long looking out there at my line.

"Think he did it?" Mat asked.

I hunched my shoulders. "I don't know, Mat."

"If he did it, you know we ought to be there, Chimley," Mat said.

I didn't answer him, but I knowed what he was talking about. I remembered the fight Mathu and Fix had out there at Marshall store. It started over a Coke bottle. After Fix had drunk his Coke, he wanted Mathu to take the empty bottle back in the store. Mathu told him he wasn't nobody's servant. Fix told him he had to take the bottle back in the store or fight.

A bunch of us was out there, white and black, sitting on the garry eating gingerbread and drinking pop. The sheriff, Guidry, was there, too. Mathu told Guidry if Fix started anything, he was go'n protect himself. Guidry went on eating his gingerbread and drinking pop like he didn't even hear him.

When Fix told Mathu to take the bottle back in the store again, and Mathu didn't, Fix hit him—and the fight was on. Worst fight I ever seen in my life. For a hour it was toe to toe. But when it was over, Mathu was up, and Fix was down. The white folks wanted to lynch Mathu, but Guidry stopped them. Then he walked up to Mathu, cracked him 'side the jaw, and Mathu hit the ground. He turned to Fix, hit him in the mouth, and Fix went down again. Then Guidry came back to the garry to finish his gingerbread and pop. That was the end of that fight. But that wasn't the last fight Mathu had on that river with them white people. And that's what Mat was talking about. That's what he meant when he said if Mathu did it we ought to be there. Mathu was the only one we knowed had ever stood up.

I looked at Mat sitting on the croker sack. He was holding the fishing pole with both hands, gazing out at the line. We had been together so much I just about knowed what he was thinking. But I asked him anyhow.

" 'Bout that bed," he said. "I'm too old to go crawling under that bed. I just don't have the strength for it no more. It's too low, Chimley."

"Mine ain't no higher," I said.

He looked at me now. A fine-featured, brown-skin man. I had knowed him all my life. Had been young men together. Had done our little running around together. Had been in a little trouble now and then, but nothing serious. Had never done what we was thinking about doing now. Maybe we had thought about it. Sure, we had thought about it. But we had never done it.

"What you say, Chimley?" he said.

I nodded to him.

We pulled in the lines and went up the bank. Mat had his fishes in the sack; mine was in the bucket.

"She want us to shoot first," I said. "I wonder why."

"I don't know," Mat said. "How's that old gun of yours working?"

"Shot good last time," I said. "That's been a while, though."

"You got any number five shells?" Mat asked.

"Might have a couple round there," I said. "I ain't looked in a long time."

"Save me one or two if you got them," Mat said. "Guess I'll have to borrow a gun, too. Nothing round my house work but that twenty-gauge and that old rifle."

"How you figuring on getting over there?" I asked him.

"Clatoo, I reckon," Mat said. "Try to hitch a ride with him on the truck."

"Have him pick me up, too," I said.

When we came up to my gate, Mat looked at me again. He was quite a bit taller than me, and I had to kinda hold my head back to look at him.

"You sure now, Chimley?" he said.

"If you go, Mat."

"I have to go, Chimley," he said. "This can be my last chance."

I looked him in the eyes. Lightish-brown eyes. They was saying much more than he had said. They was speaking for both of us, though, me and him.

"I'm going, too," I said.

Mat still looked at me. His eyes was still saying more than he had said. His eyes was saying: We wait till now? Now, when we're old men, we get to be brave?

I didn't know how to answer him. All I knowed, I had to go if he went.

Mat started toward his house, and I went on in the yard. Now, I ain't even stepped in the house good 'fore that old woman started fussing at me. What I'm doing home so early for? She don't like to be cleaning fishes this time of day. She don't like to clean fishes till evening when it's cool. I didn't answer that old woman. I set my bucket of fishes on the table in the kitchen; then I come back in the front room and got my old shotgun from against the wall. I looked through the shells I kept in a cigar box on top the armoire till I found me a number five. I blowed the dust off, loaded the old gun, stuck it out the window, turnt my head just in case the old gun decided to blow up, and I shot. Here come that old woman starting right back on me again.

"What's the matter with you, old man? What you doing shooting out that window, raising all that racket for?"

"Right now, I don't know what I'm doing all this for," I told her. "But, see, if I come back from Marshall and them fishes ain't done and ready for me to eat, I'm go'n do me some more shooting around this house. Do you hear what I'm saying?"

She tightened her mouth and rolled her eyes at me, but she had enough sense not to get too cute. I got me two or three more number five shells, blowed the dust off them, and went out to the road to wait for Clatoo.

Matthew Lincoln Brown

aka

Mat

—

When I got home I handed my sack of fishes to Ella, and I went in the other room to phone Clatoo. Emma's daughter Julie said Clatoo had just left the house, and asked me what was the matter. She said Miss Merle had called Clatoo on the phone and Clatoo had got his old shotgun and left in his truck, and she wanted me to tell her what was the matter. I told her if Clatoo didn't tell her anything, I couldn't tell her anything either, and I asked her if Clatoo told her where he was going. She said he didn't tell her nothing, but she heard him over the phone telling Miss Merle something about Mr. Billy Washington and something about Mr. Jacob Aguillard. She told me I might be able to catch him either at Silo or the old Mulatto Place, and she asked me again what was the matter.

I hung up the phone and looked up Billy Washington's number. His wife, Selina, told me Billy had just left in the truck with Clatoo. I asked her if Billy had his gun. She said yes, matter of fact he did, but how did I know? I asked her if they said where they was going next. She said she believed they was headed toward the old Mulatto Place, because she heard them saying something about Jacob Aguillard. I asked her if Jacob had a number, and she said she didn't know, but Leola Bovay had a phone. She told me if I hung on a minute she would get the number for me. When she came back on the phone, she gave me the number, and she asked me what was the matter. I hung up and called Leola's house. She told me that Clatoo had just pulled up in front of Jacob's house. She said looked like that was Billy Washington with him, and looked like both of them had shotguns. And Jacob was coming out of the house right now, and he had a shotgun, too. I told her to run out on the garry and tell Clatoo to wait a second. I heard her putting the phone down, then a little while later picking it up again. She said Clatoo was waiting. I asked her if she had a twelve-gauge shotgun that could shoot. She told me when her husband died he had left two or three old guns around there, but she couldn't tell one gauge from another, and she asked me again what was the matter. I told her to take the guns out to Clatoo and ask Clatoo to check them, and if he found a twelve-gauge that could shoot, bring it. I asked her if she had any number five shells, and she said she didn't know. I told her to get all the shells she had and take them out to Clatoo, and tell Clatoo to pick out some and bring them. She asked me what was the matter. I told her to tell Clatoo to tell her, because I didn't know nothing. I hung up. When I looked around, I saw Ella standing in the door with her hands on her hips. So big she was filling up that whole door.

"What's all this about shotguns?" she asked.

"We going hunting," I said.

"Going hunting what this time of day?"

"Just hunting," I said.

"Matthew, I'm talking to you," she said. "Hunting what?"

"I'll tell you when I get back," I said.

"You telling me 'fore you leave from here," she said.

"Go somewhere and sit down, woman," I said. "This men business."

"I'm making it my business," she said, coming up to me. "Hunting what?"

"Get out of my face, woman," I said. "For once in my life 'fore I die, I'm go'n—" I stopped. "Just don't be asking me no questions," I said, and went out on the garry.

I heard her in there on the phone; then she hung up, and I could hear her dialing somebody else. Then I heard her screaming, "What? What? Uncle Billy? What?" I heard her slamming the phone down and coming out on the garry.

"What's Uncle Billy doing with a shotgun old as he is?"

"How do I know?" I said. "I don't keep Billy Washington in my pocket."

"You know, all right," she said, her hands on her hips again. "You know, all right. And you go'n tell me 'fore you leave from here."

I turned on her. "You want to know, huh?" I said. "You want to know, huh?"

Now she started backing way from me, like she thought I was go'n hit her.

"I'll tell you," I said. "A Cajun's dead over there at Marshall. Laying on his back in Mathu's yard. Now you know."

"And what's that got to do with you?" she said. She was safe enough away so she could talk big again. "And what's that got to do with Uncle Billy?"

"You mean you still don't know?" I asked her.

I turned from her and looked up the road. But Clatoo still wasn't coming yet.

"You old fool," she said. "You old fool. Y'all gone crazy?"

"That's right," I said, looking up the road, not at her. "Anytime we say we go'n stand up for something, they say we crazy. You right, we all gone crazy."

"You old fool," she said. "You old fool. If I can't stop you, I bet you I'll call your brother. He'll stop you."

"You and Jesse both better stay out of my way if you know what's good for you," I said, looking up the road. Clatoo still wasn't coming.

"If you think I'm go'n let you go to Marshall and get yourself kilt—"

"You can't stop me, that's for sure," I said, looking up the road.

"I'll call the law," she said. "You won't listen to me or your brother, I bet you the law'll make you listen."

I turned back on her, pointing my finger at her.

"You touch that phone, woman, somebody'll be patching your head."

"Just wait," she said, going back inside.

I caught up with her and pushed on her, but she was too big for me to push her clean out of the way. But I beat her to the phone, and I jerked it out of the wall and throwed it down on the floor.

"Now call with that," I said.

"You old fool," she said. "You old fool. What's the matter with you, you old fool?"

My chest started heaving, heaving, just heaving. Like I had been running up a hill, a steep hill, and now I had reached the top. I looked at that woman I had been living with all these years like I didn't even know who she was. My chest heaving, and me just looking at her like I didn't know who she was. Something in my face made her back back from me. She kept backing back, backing back, till she had touched the wall. I kept looking at her like I didn't know who she was. My chest heaving, just heaving.

"What's the matter with me? Woman, what's the matter with me? All these years we been living together, woman, you still don't know what's the matter with me? The years we done struggled in George Medlow's field, making him richer and richer and us getting poorer and poorer—and you still don't know what's the matter with me? The years I done stood out in that back yard and cussed at God, the years I done stood out on that front garry and cussed the world, the times I done come home drunk and beat you for no reason at all—and, woman, you still don't know what's the matter with me? Oliver, woman!" I screamed at her. "Oliver. How they let him die in the hospital just 'cause he was black. No doctor to serve him, let him bleed to death, 'cause he was black. And you ask me what's the matter with me?"

I stopped now and looked at her. I could feel the hot tears running down my face. I pressed my lips, I could feel my mouth trembling, but the tears kept on running down my face. It had been a long time since I had talked to her like this. A longer time since she had seen me crying. I didn't turn my head. I didn't wipe my face. I just stood there looking at her. At first she looked scared. Then it turned to hate—hate 'cause she was so scared.

"He works in mysterious ways," I told her. "Give a old nigger like me one more chance to do something with his life. He gived me that chance, and I'm taking it, I'm going to Marshall. Even if I have to die at Marshall. I know I'm old, maybe even crazy, but I'm going anyhow. And it ain't nothing you can do about it. Pray if you want to. Pray for all us old fools. But don't try to stop me. So help me, God, woman, don't try to stop me."

I heard Clatoo out there blowing, and I wiped my face and went out on the garry. Clatoo was in that old green pickup truck he used for peddling his garden. He had on that little narrow-brim straw, a white shirt, and a bow tie. Clatoo always let you know he was a businessman.

In the front with him was Billy Washington and Jacob Aguillard. Billy was from Silo, Jacob from the old Mulatto

Place. Jacob and his kind didn't have too much to do with darker people, but he was here today.

In the back of the truck was Chimley and Cherry Bello. Cherry was between red and yellow, with a lot of brown curly hair. I got in the back there with him and Chimley. While Clatoo turned the truck around, Ella came out on the garry to watch us.

"Y'all had a round, huh?" Cherry asked me.

"She didn't want me to go," I said.

"I was at the store when I got the call," Cherry said. "Mine don't know a thing about it. And I sure wasn't go'n call and tell her."

Cherry Bello owned a liquor-and-grocery store on the highway between Silo and Baton Rouge.

"I just told mine my food better be ready when I got back home," Chimley said. "She don't know where I'm going. I don't think she even care."

We was sitting on the floor, backs against the cab, and feet toward the tailgate. Cherry Bello had two twelve-gauge shotguns on the floor 'side him, and he handed me one of them. He handed me couple of shells, too.

"Leola sent that," he said.

"Y'all shot?" I asked.

"I shot," Chimley said.

"I'm saving mine till we hit the field," Cherry said. "Might see me a rabbit. No use wasting a good bullet on nothing."

"What we go'n do in the field?" I asked him.

"Clatoo go'n drop us off just before he reach Marshall," Cherry said. "We go'n walk across the field, and come in from the back. Clatoo got another load he got to go pick up. Look like a lot of people want to gather at Marshall today."

"Sure do," Chimley said quietly.

Chimley was sitting in the middle. He was smaller than me and Cherry Bello. Blacker than me and Cherry, too, that's why we all called him Chimley. He didn't mind his friends calling him Chimley, 'cause he knowed we didn't mean nothing. But he sure didn't like them white folks calling him Chimley. He was always telling them that his daddy had named him Robert Louis Stevenson Banks, not Chimley. But all they did was laugh at him, and they went on calling him Chimley anyhow.

I looked at him sitting there between me and Cherry. He was my old partner, my old fishing partner. Had knowed Chimley for years and years. My closest friend now, with all the others dead and gone.

"How you feel there, old buddy?" I said to him.

He looked at me and grinned. "Scared," he said. He had on that old Dodgers' baseball cap that he had had since the Dodgers was in Brooklyn. It had faded to a light light blue, and it was too big for his head. But old Chimley was a Dodgers' fan down to his heart. "I'm scared, but I'm here," he said.

I nodded and grinned back at him. I was scared, too. But at the same time I felt kinda good, knowing me and Chimley and Cherry, and all the rest of us, was doing something different, for the first time.

Grant Bello

aka

Cherry

Yank was waiting for us behind a bush on the river-bank side of the road. Clatoo didn't have to stop, just slow down, and old Yank hopped in the back of the truck. Yank was in his early seventies, but he still thought he was a cowboy. He used to break horses and mules thirty, forty years ago, and he still wore the same kinda clothes he wore back then. His straw hat was draped like a cowboy hat. Wore a faded red polka-dotted handkerchief, tied in a loose knot round his neck. His pants legs was stucked down in his rubber boots—not cowboy boots. Back, shoulders had been broke I don't know how many times; made him walk leaning forward. Hands had been broke and rebroke; now he couldn't shut them too tight, or open them too wide. But he still thought he was a cowboy. He spoke when he first got in the truck, but after that we didn't do much talking. We was just feeling proud. I could see it on Yank's face; I could feel it sitting next to Chimley and Mat. Proud as we could be.

A mile or so after we picked up Yank, we picked up Dirty Red at Talbot. Clatoo had to blow the horn twice before we

saw Dirty Red shuffling from behind the house. He carried
the old shotgun by the barrel, the stock almost touching the
ground. He had a self-rolled cigarette hanging from the corner
of his mouth. He had as much ashes hanging on the cigarette
as the cigarette was long. Dirty Red wouldn't take time to
knock the ashes off a cigarette. Ashes fell off when it couldn't
hang on any longer. Dirty Red got in the truck and spoke to
everybody.

"Hoa," he said. We greeted him back. He looked at Chimley. "What's happening there, Chimley?"

Chimley nodded. Dirty Red grinned at him.

Three or four miles after we picked up Dirty Red, Clatoo
turned off the main highway, down a dirt road that separated Morgan and Marshall plantations. There was cane
on both sides, Morgan on one side, Marshall on the other.
The cane was so tall the blades hung over the ditches and
over the road. After going a little ways so the people on
the highway couldn't see us, Clatoo stopped the truck
and told us to get out. He had to go farther up the highway for another load. He told us to wait for them at the
graveyard, and we would all walk up to Mathu's house
together. He thought that would look better than if we
straggled in one or two at a time. He turned the truck
around and headed back to the highway, and we started
walking.

Jacob and Mat was in front, Chimley right behind them.
Jacob had his gun over his shoulder, carrying it like a soldier.
Mat had his tucked under his arm, barrel pointed toward the
ground, like a hunter. Chimley had his under his arm, too,
but he didn't walk nearly as straight as Mat or Jacob. Just
shuffling along, head down, like he was following their tracks
in the dust. If they had made a quick stop, Chimley woulda
butt into them, I'm sure. Me and Yank followed Chimley,
with Dirty Red and Billy Washington behind us. Billy carried
his gun over his shoulder, but carried it too loosely. More like

he was carrying a stick of wood than a gun. Billy couldn't hit the broad side of a barn if he stood two feet in front of it. Next to him, Dirty Red was nearly dragging his gun in the dust. I don't know who looked worse, Dirty Red, Billy Washington, or Chimley. Neither one of them looked like he was ready for battle, that's for sure.

We still had cane, tall and blue-green, on both sides of the road. Morgan on the left, Marshall on the right. But it wasn't Marshall cane anymore. Beau Boutan was leasing the plantation from the Marshall family. Beau and his family had been leasing all the land the past twenty-five, thirty years. The very same land we had worked, our people had worked, our people's people had worked since the time of slavery. Now Mr. Beau had it all. Or, I should say, he had it all up to about twelve o'clock that day.

After about half a mile, we turned right on another headland. You had cane here, too, but just on one side. On the left the cane had been cut and hauled away, and you could see all the way back to the swamps. It made me feel lonely. In my old age, specially in grinding, when I saw an empty cane field, it always made me feel lonely. The rows looked so naked and gray and lonely—like an old house where the people have moved from. Where good friends have moved from, leaving the house empty and bare, with nothing but ghosts now to keep it company.

I was still looking across the field when I heard the shot. I turned just in time to see a little rabbit bobbing across the empty rows. By the time I took aim, he was already down one of the middles, and all I could see was his little ears bobbing every now and then. I looked back at Billy and Dirty Red. Billy was just bringing the gun down from his shoulder. Me and Yank waited for him and Dirty Red to catch up.

"Missed him, huh, Billy?" I asked.

Billy didn't answer. He wouldn't even look at me or Yank. He was too 'shamed.

"I hope he don't miss Fix like that," Dirty Red teased Billy. Dirty Red had a cigarette hanging from the corner of his mouth, and he helt his head a little to the side to keep the smoke out his eyes. "Rabbit was so close I started to hit him in the head with the butt of my gun, but I wanted Billy to have him."

"He was moving," Billy said. He said it quietly. He wouldn't look at us.

"After you stumbled over him, he started moving," Dirty Red teased Billy.

Billy kept his head down.

"You'll get another chance, Billy, you just wait," I told him.

We started walking again. Me and Yank in front, and Billy and Dirty Red following us. Mat, Jacob, and Chimley had stopped for a second, and started walking again. Behind us, I could hear Dirty Red laughing. He would be quiet a second, then laugh again. I knowed he was still laughing at Billy. I hoped Billy missing that rabbit wasn't a bad sign for the rest of that day.

Now, up ahead, I could see the pecan and oak trees in the graveyard at Marshall. You had a dozen trees spread out over the graveyard, and about that same number of headstones, maybe two or three more. But twenty-five, thirty years ago you didn't have more than two or three headstones in there all total. Back there when I was growing up, people didn't even mark the graves. Each family had a little plot, and everybody knowed where that little plot was. If it was a big family, then they had to have a little bit more, sometimes from the plot of a smaller family. But who cared? They had all come from the same place, they had mixed together when they was alive, so what's the difference if they mixed together now? That old graveyard had been the burial ground for black folks ever since the time of slavery. I was seventy-four, and I had grandparents in there.

We squatted under a pecan tree just outside the graveyard fence. You had pecans on the ground all around you, and if you looked up you could see them hanging loose in the shells. The next good wind or rain was go'n bring them all down. It was a good year for pecans.

We hadn't been there more than ten, maybe fifteen minutes when Jacob stood up and went inside the graveyard. I looked back over my shoulder, and I seen him pulling up weeds from Tessie's grave. Tessie was his sister. She was one of them great big pretty mulatto gals who messed around with the white man and the black man. The white men wanted her all for themself, and they told her to stay away from the niggers. But she didn't listen, and they killed her. Ran her through the quarters out into that St. Charles River—Mardi Gras Day, 1947.

But listen to this now. Her own people at the old Mulatto Place wouldn't even take her body home. They was against her living here in the first place round the darker people. I'm not dark myself, I'm light as them, but I'm not French, not quality. Them, they're quality, them; but they wouldn't even take her body home. Buried her with the kind she had lived with. Maybe that's why Jacob was here today, to make up for what he had done his sister over thirty years ago. After pulling up the weeds, he knelt down at the head of the grave and made the sign of the cross. Next thing you knowed, every last one of us was in there visiting our people's graves.

You had to walk in grass knee-high to reach some of the graves. The people usually cleaned up the graveyard if they had to bury somebody, or for La Toussaint. But nobody had been buried there in a good while, and La Toussaint wasn't for another month, so you had grass, weeds everywhere. Pecans and acorns—you could feel them under your feet, you could hear them crack when you stepped on them.

We went to our different little family plots. But we wasn't too sure about all the graves. If they had been put there the last twenty, twenty-five years, yes, then we could tell for sure. But, say, if they had been put there forty, fifty years ago, it was no way we could tell if we was looking at the right grave for the right person. Most of the graves after a while had just shifted and mixed with all the others.

Dirty Red was a little bit farther away from the rest of us, more over into the corner. We had never mixed too well with his people. We thought they was too trifling, never doing anything for themself. Dirty Red was the last one. Maybe that's why he was here today, to do something for all the others. But maybe that's why we was all there, to do something for the others.

After I had knelt down and prayed over my own family plot, I wandered over to where Dirty Red was standing all by himself. He was eating a pecan and looking down at the weeds that covered the graves. Dirty Red hadn't knelt down or pulled one weed from one grave. Some of the graves was all sunked in.

"My brother Gabe there," Dirty Red said. I didn't know for sure what spot he was looking at, because soon as he said it he cracked another pecan with his teeth. Not cracking couple of them together in his hand, but cracking them one at a time with his teeth. "My mon, Jude; my pa, François, right there," he said. I still didn't know for sure where he was looking. "Uncle Ned right in there—somewhere," he said.

The whole place was all sunked in, and you had weeds everywhere, so I couldn't tell for sure where Dirty Red was looking. I never looked at his eyes to see if they shifted from one spot to another. But, knowing Dirty Red, I figured they probably didn't. That woulda been too much like work. Even to bat his eyes was too much work for Dirty Red.

"You got plenty of us in here," I said, looking around the graveyard. I could see Mat, Chimley, Yank—all of them standing near their people's graves. "This where you want them to bring you?" I asked Dirty Red.

"Might as well, if it's still here," he said.

"They getting rid of these old graveyards more and more," I said. "These white folks coming up today don't have no respect for the dead."

Dirty Red cracked another pecan with his teeth.

"Graveyard pecan always taste good," he said. "You tried any of them?"

"I'll gather me up a few before we leave," I said.

I looked out on the empty field on the other side of the fence. The cane rows came up to twenty or thirty feet of the graveyard. Beau had cut and hauled the cane away, and I could see all the way back to the swamps. Them long old lonely cane rows took me back back, I can tell you that.

"Him and Charlie had a chance to get some of it done," I said to Dirty Red.

"He sure won't be getting no more done," Dirty Red said.

"What you think of all this, Dirty Red?" I asked him.

"Well, I look at it this way," he said. "How many more years I got here on this old earth?"

That was all he had to say. He stopped right there. Just like Dirty Red not to finish something. That woulda taken too much of his strength, and him and his people believed in saving as much strength as they could.

"With that little time left, you thought you ought to do something worthwhile with your life?" I asked, trying to coax him on.

"Something like that," he said. He ate another pecan.

"Your people will be proud of you, Dirty Red."

"I reckon lot of them in here go'n be proud after this day is over," he said. "Might have some of us joining them, too."

"You think it might come to that?"

"That's up to Fix," he said. He looked at me and grinned. Then he looked past me and nodded. "Here come Clatoo and them."

They came down the road, where the old railroad tracks

used to be. Clatoo was in front, with his gun in one hand and a shoe box under his left arm. Bing and Ding Lejeune from the Two Indian Bayou was a step behind him. Both had on khakis and both had on straw hats, and you had to get right on them to tell who was who, and if you didn't know Ding had the scar 'cross the left side of his face, you still couldn't tell which one you was talking to. Clabber Hornsby, the albino from Jarreau, came behind Bing and Ding Lejeune, walking by himself. Clabber's head and face from this distance was all one color—white white. What he had a gun for, only God knows. He couldn't stop blinking long enough to sight, let alone kill somebody. Behind Clabber came Jean Pierre Ricord and Gable Rauand. Now, that was somebody, Gable, I never woulda expected to see. He very seldomed ever left home. To church, maybe, but that was about all. Behind him and Jean Pierre came Cedrick Tucker and Sidney Brooks. Cedrick's brother Silas was the last black sharecropper on the place. He was buried here. Walking next to Cedrick was Sidney Brooks—we all called him Coot. Old Coot was in his World War I uniform. Even had on the cap, and the belt 'cross his shoulder. He carried his gun 'cross the other shoulder in a soldier's manner. We left the graveyard to meet them. We met under the pecan tree, and couple of the fellows squatted down against the wire fence.

"Everybody shot?" Clatoo asked soon as he walked up.

"Billy shot at a rabbit on his foot and missed him," Dirty Red said. Dirty Red was squatting by the fence.

Couple of the fellows laughed at Dirty Red.

"That rabbit was moving, Dirty Red," Billy told him. "But you ain't, and don't forget it."

The men laughed again. Not loud. Quiet. Thoughtful. More from nervousness than anything else.

"Save your fighting for later," Clatoo told Billy Washington. "Them ain't shot, shoot," he said. "She told us to bring empty shells."

"What we suppose to do with them empties, throw them at Fix?" I asked Clatoo.

"You can ask her that when you get there," Clatoo said. "Them ain't shot yet, shoot up in them trees. Let them down there hear you."

Five or six of us raised our guns and shot. A few pecans, a few acorns, some moss and leaves fell down on the sunked-in graves under the trees.

"Anybody got anything to say 'fore we get started?" Clatoo asked. "Anybody feel like turning around? It can get a little hot out there today. Anybody?"

Nobody said they wanted to turn around.

"All right," Clatoo said. "Let's get moving. Heads up and backs straight. We going in like soldiers, not like tramps. All right?"

He started out first, gun in one hand, shoe box under his arm. Mat and Jacob followed, then the rest of us. Jean Pierre, Billy Washington, and Chimley was doing all they could to walk with their heads up and backs straight.

Cyril Robillard

aka

Clatoo

Candy met us at the gate, where the gate used to be; you didn't have a fence or a gate there now. She stood on one side the ditch, we was on the other side. She was a little, spare woman, not too tall; always wearing pants and shirts, never dresses. She thanked us for coming. You could tell by her face how happy she was to see us. Thanking this one, thanking that one, thanking the other one. She knowed most of us by name, because we all lived in the same parish and she had traveled all over the parish all her life. After everybody had spoke to her, she looked back at me. She knowed about me and my gardening, and she figured I had brought the people there in my truck. Now she started telling me what had happened. I listened good, but I could see from the start she was lying. For one thing, I knowed what Mathu meant to that family, and specially to her. Besides that, she was trying too hard to make me believe her. Like most of these white folks you'll find round here, when they trying to convince you they'll look you dead in the eye, daring you to think otherwise from what they want you to think. Adding to all that, she told it too fast, too pat—she had practiced it too much.

After listening to her, I looked at Mathu squatting against the wall with the gun in his arms. He wasn't looking at us, he was looking over us toward the trees on the other side of the road. He acted like he didn't care if we was even there. Mathu was one of them blue-black Singaleese niggers. Always bragged about not having no white man's blood in his veins. He looked down on all the rest of us who had some, and the more you had, the more he looked down on you. I was brown-skinned—my grandpa white, my grandma Indian and black, and both my parents black; so he didn't look down on me quite as much as he did some others, like Jacob, or Cherry, or the Lejeune brothers. With Clabber and Rooster, he just shook his head. Rooster was yellow, with nappy black hair; Clabber was milk white, with nappy white hair. Mathu just shook his head when he saw either one of them.

We moved in the yard and made a circle round Beau laying there in the grass. His mouth and eyes still opened, his face caked with dust, his brown hair full of grass seeds. The shotgun pellets had hit him on the left side of his chest, tearing off that part of his shirt. Flies covered the dried blood.

After looking at him, I went over and shook hands with Rufe Seaberry, Johnny Paul, and Rooster Jackson standing by the garden fence. We didn't have much to say, just a nod, but in that nod I could see how proud they was to be there.

Glo Hebert, Hazel Robinson, and Rooster's big wife, Beulah Jackson, was all sitting on the steps. Glo had her three little grandchildren next to her side. I went to shake hands but I had to pass by Reverend Jameson first. He was the preacher in the quarters, and he was the only man there who didn't have a gun, and the only person there who looked like he hated the sight of us. When I shook Glo's hand, she helt on to mine awhile. I knowed why she did it—two reasons. One, she was worried about what might happen if Fix came there. But, two, she was proud of us all being there now.

I shook hands with Hazel and Beulah, and I spoke to Corrine, sitting in the rocking chair on the garry. Sitting there straight and lifeless as a scarecrow. She didn't speak or nod, just gazed out there in the yard, at nobody, at nothing. I went to the end of the garry and spoke to Mathu.

"You all right?" I asked him.

"I'm all right," he said, not looking at me.

I went around the house and hid the shoe box behind the second block under the house. When I came back, I raised up two fingers to Mat Brown, and he nodded back. I sat at the end of the garry and looked at Mathu. The rest of the men had moved to different parts of the yard. Some was standing over by the garden talking; some was standing next to the end of the garry. Dirty Red and a couple more squatted on the walk. Candy had come back in the yard, and she was standing next to the steps where Glo sat with her grandchildren. And standing away from everybody else, all to himself, was that preacher Jameson. He looked from one of us to another, from one to another. He wanted to say something, but he didn't know where to start.

"Well?" I said to Mathu.

"She called y'all, I didn't." He didn't look at me; he was looking toward the tractor out there in the road. The motor was still running, but he wasn't paying it any 'tention. He was looking over the tractor, over the trailers of cane, toward the trees in that far pasture. "When the man get here, I'll turn myself in," he said.

"You mean I'm go'n turn myself in, don't you?" Johnny Paul said, from over by the garden. Johnny Paul had the shotgun tucked under his arm, the barrel flat against his leg. "You ain't taking no credit for what I did."

"You go'n have to come after me," Rufe said. He was standing next to Johnny Paul by the garden.

"Y'all better fit me in there somewhere," Mat said, across the yard from them.

"How could you shoot him? You don't even stay here," Johnny Paul said.

"Chicken hawk," Mat said. He looked up at the sky. The sky was clear blue, not a cloud anywhere. But still a little too warm for October. "Can't keep that bugger from eating my chickens for nothing in the world. Told Chimley this morning I was go'n take my shotgun and go looking for that rascal. Followed him all the way from Medlow to Marshall. Never could get a clean shot at that bugger." He was still looking up at the sky, like he thought the chicken hawk might fly over his head.

"He sure told me that," Chimley said. He looked up at the sky, too. He even stepped back and looked up into that pecan tree behind Mathu's house. "That's how I happened to get my gun and went out looking for that old chicken hawk, too."

"I didn't see neither one of y'all," Bing Lejeune said. Him and his brother Ding was standing on the other side of the walk from Chimley. "I been here talking to Mathu all morning long, and I didn't—"

"I didn't even see you," Ding said.

"But you see this, don't you?" Bing said, raising his fist playfully.

"You see this one?" Ding said, raising his fist. "Don't make me mad now. You know me when I get mad."

"Sure, sure," Bing said. "But you can't hit the broad side of a barn with a cannon. Everybody on the bayou know that."

The rest of the people said pretty much the same. One claimed he did it, then another one; one, then another one. Clabber, Jean Pierre, Billy, Rooster, Coot—one after the other. Dirty Red, squatting on the walk, took the cigarette from his mouth and blowed off the ashes. No, he didn't do it right away. He waited for it to fall off. When it didn't, he blowed it off. He frowned at the ashes before he did it. Then he looked up.

"You boys ain't go'n take this from me now, is you?" he asked the rest of us.

"Look like you go'n have to get in line to shoot Beau, Dirty Red," Cherry Bello told him.

Dirty Red looked at his cigarette and tapped it lightly before he put it back in his mouth.

"Maybe me and Old Hanna might have to do some more shooting, 'liminate some of the competition," he said. "What you say about that, old gal?" he said to his shotgun. "Ready to 'liminate some of the competition?"

While all this was going on, I could see Jameson getting madder and madder. Jameson was a short, jet-black, bald-headed little fellow with a white mustache and beard. That bald head was shining in that hot sun like a looking glass.

"Y'all will sing a different tune before this day is over with," he said. "Just mark my word."

"I've already told you to go on home, Reverend Jameson," Candy said, from the other side of the steps. "I've been telling you for the last hour—you don't want to be here, go on home. I don't want to have to tell you anymore."

"This is my place, Candy," Jameson said. "I ain't got no home if they burn this place down." He turned to the rest of us, beads of sweat just popping out of his head and running down his face. "Can't y'all understand what I'm trying to say to y'all?" he asked us.

Nobody answered him. He looked from one to another, from one to another, but nobody answered him. Most of the people wouldn't even look back at him. He came closer to the garry.

"Mathu, for God's sake, go turn yourself in," he pleaded with Mathu. "Please, Mathu."

Mathu looked over Jameson's head toward the trees in that far pasture. He didn't answer.

Jameson came round the end of the garry where I was sitting. He was crying now. He was pressing his lips tight, but I could see the tears running down his face.

"Clatoo," he said. "You got sense. Talk to him. Tell him what can happen."

I didn't answer him. I didn't want to look at him. I looked at the tractor out there in the road. The motor still running.

"Clatoo, please," Jameson said. "Please."

"I come here to stand, not to talk," I said, not looking at him.

But he kept on looking at me. Just standing there crying, his mouth pressed tight, looking at me.

"That's what y'all come here for?" he asked. "To die? Y'all think that'll make up for all the hurt? That's what y'all think?"

I didn't answer him. I didn't look at him. I could see him from the corner of my eyes crying, his mouth pressed tight again.

Now he looked at Candy.

"You satisfied now?" he asked her. "You satisfied now? You think you doing him any good if you soak this land with blood?"

She didn't answer him, either. He kept on looking at her. I could see it out the corner of my eyes. But she wasn't paying him any more 'tention than anybody else did. He turned back on the rest of the people.

"Go home, old fools," he said. "Old fools, go home."

But nobody paid him any mind.

For the next few seconds, everything was quiet, 'cept for that tractor out there in the road. Somewhere in the swamps a owl called, but after that—nothing. Then a pecan dropped from that tree in the back yard, fell on the tin roof, and tumbled to the ground. We all looked at it there a second; then Snookum went to pick it up. Dirty Red, squatting on the walk, gave the little boy a handful of pecans from his pocket.

The boy went back to the steps and gave some of the pecans to the other two children. They started eating.

"Well, Candy?" I said, looking at her by the steps.

She turned to look at me.

"What now?" I said.

"Did everybody shoot?" she asked.

"We shot. We kept the empty shells."

"All number fives?"

"Number fives," I said.

"You know why, don't you, Clatoo?"

I nodded my head. She looked at me awhile; then she glanced at Mathu and faced the road again. You'd do anything in the world for him, wouldn't you? Wouldn't you? I thought to myself.

Jameson had been watching her, too, and now he saw another chance to break in.

"And what's that suppose to do, fool Mapes?" he asked her. When she didn't answer him, he turned to me. "Y'all think Mapes that crazy? The man on his back right here in Mathu's yard, the tractor out there still running, right in front of Mathu's house. Some of y'all live far as Silo, the old Mulatto Place, Bayonne—ten, twelve miles from here. Don't y'all know Mapes go'n know half of y'all couldn't be nowhere near this place when this happened? Y'all all gone plumb crazy?"

"Reverend Jameson, just shut up," Beulah said. "Just shut up. Nobody listening to you; so just shut up. Go on back home, like Candy said. Nobody listening to you today."

"Maybe I ought to shoot him," Rooster said. "You think I ought to shoot him, Dirty Red?"

"No, let him slide," Dirty Red said. "He might change 'fore the shooting start."

Couple of the men laughed at Rooster and Dirty Red.

It was quiet for a while; then we saw the dust. We couldn't see the car, just the dust coming down the quarters high over the weeds. We all thought it was Mapes, till the car pulled up and stopped. Through the naked bean poles in Mathu's garden, through the weeds and bushes on the ditch bank, I could make out that little blue sports car that Candy's boyfriend owned. She went out in the road to meet him. The rest of us settled back again.

Louis Alfred
Dimoulin

aka

Lou Dimes

Now what I was trying to figure out was who in Marshall Quarters could—not would—kill Beau Boutan. There were nothing but old people there. The young ones had all gone away, leaving only the old and a few children. So who could do it? Not Charlie. Too many times I had seen Beau speak to him as you would speak to a dog, and he would not raise his head, let alone his voice. Then who? Janey was too hysterical to make any sense over the telephone when I called the house. All she could say was hurry up and get there because Candy needed me. *Candy needed me?* I had been knowing Candy for three years, and during all that time I had never known her to need anybody.

I drove the thirty-five miles from Baton Rouge to Marshall in exactly thirty minutes. Why I didn't have every highway patrolman in the state of Louisiana on my tail was just a miracle. When I came up even with Marshall House, I saw the Major's and Miss Merle's cars in the yard. Candy's big LTD was not on the lawn in front of the door, so I figured she was still in the quarters where Janey had said she was.

The length of the quarters was little less than half a mile, beginning with the highway and going back into the fields. The bushes and weeds grew so tall on either side of the road that the road seemed no wider than a king-size bed sheet. Somewhere down there I could make out a tractor and a car. As I came deeper into the quarters, I noticed that there were no people around. The doors and windows of the few old houses were open, but no one sat out on the porches, and no one stood in the yard or worked the gardens. The place looked as if everyone had suddenly picked up and gone. Knowing the past reputation of Beau's family, I figured that was the smartest thing to do.

I had barely stopped the car when I saw Candy coming out into the road. She seemed calm, not nearly as excited as I thought she should be. Surely not nearly as worried as I was.

"I'm glad you got here," she said.

"What happened?" I asked after getting out of the car.

"Over there," she said, nodding back over her shoulder.

I looked in that direction, but I couldn't see a thing for the weeds and bushes along the ditch bank.

"What happened, Candy?" I asked her again.

"I killed him," she said, looking me straight in the eye. She turned to go back into the yard, but I grabbed her arm.

"What did you say?"

"I killed Beau," she said, and pulled her arm free.

I stood there a moment. I could feel my heart pounding, pounding; no, not only could I feel it pounding, I could hear it trying to jump out of my chest. I shook my head. No, I hadn't heard what I thought I had heard, and I went after her. But I had only gone to the front of her car when I suddenly stopped again. Like I had run into a brick wall. It was a wall, all right, but a wall twenty, thirty feet away from me. Not a wall of brick, stone, or wood, but a wall of old black men with shotguns. I don't know how many there were—fifteen, eighteen of them; standing, squatting, sitting—scattered all over the place. And waiting. Waiting. But not for me. That was obvious. Some of them acted as though I was not even there.

When I felt it was safe to go into the yard, I crossed the ditch over to where Candy was standing. At her feet lay Beau Boutan, his mouth and eyes still open, his face caked with sweat and dirt, his dark brown hair speckled with dry grass seeds. He was about thirty, roughly handsome, maybe a hundred and seventy-five pounds. He wore khaki pants and khaki shirt and cowboy boots. His straw hat, bottom side up, lay in the weeds a few feet over to my left. A shotgun lay in the weeds a couple of steps to my right. I stooped over and picked up a thick, hairy, sweat-and-dirt-caked wrist, held it a moment, and dropped it back down. A half-dozen flies flew away from the coagulated blood on his chest, but came back almost immediately.

I stood up and looked around at the people again. Not one had said a single word or moved an inch. Some were looking at me, most were not. I stared at the one nearest me. He could have been in his seventies, but sometimes it's hard to estimate their ages. He looked about the average age of all the others with guns. He wore overalls and a denim shirt, an ageless gray felt hat, brogans laced with cowhide, but no socks.

"Um the one," he said.

Not with anger. Not threatening. If proud, not boasting. Simply, without my asking, "Um the one."

I looked at another one. He was squatting over by the garden fence smoking a cigarette. With the stock of the gun on the ground and the barrel across his knee, he was looking out at the tractor in the road. He showed so much more interest in that damned tractor than he did me that I almost turned around to look at the damned thing again myself.

"You there?"

He nodded. He must have had great lateral vision, because he knew I was talking to him without ever looking in my direction.

"I kilt him," he said.

I picked out another one sitting on the bottom step with his head bowed. He was tapping the stock of the gun against a brick in the ground. I wondered if that damned gun was loaded.

"You on the step?"

He didn't stop tapping the brick for a second. Didn't even raise his head.

"Yes, sir, I did it."

I see, I thought; I see. All heroes, huh?

I looked at the preacher standing away from the rest. Pathetic, bald, weary-looking little man. He was the only one there who seemed frightened. He was sweating, probably from arguing with them.

"Can you tell me what's going on down here, Reverend Jameson?"

"You better ask her, Mr. Lou," he said, nodding toward Candy. "She done already told me to shut up or go home."

I turned back to Candy, who was standing only a couple of feet behind me.

"Well?"

"Well what?" she said, looking up at me.

"Didn't you hear them?"

"I heard them."

"You still say you did it?"

"I did it."

"You're lying, Candy. You know I know you're lying."

She got angry now. She told me she didn't care whether I believed her or not. She told me that Charlie and Beau had gotten into a fight back there in the fields, and Charlie had run up here to Mathu's house. She was here talking to Mathu.

Charlie had been here only a minute or two when Beau came after him with a shotgun. She told him not to come into the yard, he did, and she took Mathu's gun and shot him. She said she didn't care who didn't believe her, that's the way it happened.

"And what are they doing here?" I asked her.

"To protect me, I suppose."

"Since when?"

She couldn't answer that. I looked down at Beau, at the flies gathered on his chest.

"Can't somebody at least bring something out here to cover him up?" I said.

"Corrine," Candy called to the woman on the porch. "Go inside and get me a sheet or something."

Corrine, wearing a gray dress that could have been blue or purple once, got up from the rocker and went inside the house. A moment later she returned carrying a bedspread that could have been green, pink, blue, or purple once, but now it, too, had faded to a dull gray like the dress that she wore. She reached it toward one of the men nearest the porch, and he brought it to me. I watched him as he came toward me, but he avoided my eyes. After passing me the spread, he returned to the porch to take his post.

"You called Mapes?" I asked Candy.

"Miss Merle was down here," she said. "I told her to call him after you went by."

"For God's sake, Candy, before Mapes gets here, tell me the truth. Did Mathu do this?"

"I've already told you the truth," she said. "I did it."

"Fix is going to demand a nigger's blood, Candy. You know that, don't you?"

She came up closer to me, her head even with my chest, her eyes blazing, her mouth trembling she was so angry.

"I killed that son of a bitch," she said. "That's what I'm

going to tell Mapes, what I'm going to tell radio, what I'm going to give television. I killed that son of a bitch. Now, I called you here because I need you to stand beside me. Because I don't have anybody else. Nobody else. But if you don't want to stay, you can go on back to Baton Rouge. I don't beg."

We stared at each other. She could see I didn't believe a damned thing she had said. The longer we looked at each other, the angrier she became. Her mouth tightened into a straight line. She wanted to hit, but she held back. She knew she still needed me.

I turned from her to look at those old fools around me. I didn't know who I felt the most pity for. I knew she hadn't done it, and she would get out of it. But somebody had to pay for Beau's lying there.

They saw the dust before I did. When I looked over my shoulder, Mapes had already stopped out in front of the house. He was sitting on the passenger side of the black Ford Fairlane, one of his deputies driving. They sat there watching us about a minute before getting out of the car. Mapes got out slowly, as though he was very tired. He was about my height, six three, six four, but he outweighed me by a hundred pounds at least. He was in his late sixties. He wore a gray lightweight suit, a gray hat, white shirt, and a red tie. His deputy, who wore a beige suit and tie but no hat, got out on the other side. He seemed to be in his early twenties. He was about five eight, and weighed round a hundred and forty pounds. Even from this distance you could see he was scared. He was unarmed, and he reached back into the car for a gun. Mapes spoke to him from over his shoulder, and he put the gun back.

Mapes took off his hat and wiped the sweatband with a handkerchief; then he wiped his forehead, the sides and the back of his neck; then he put the hat back on his head, and the handkerchief back into his pocket. He did all that while watching us. He turned his head, not his body, to check out the tractor whose motor was still running. Thirty seconds of this, and he looked back at us again. He raised his hand to his mouth and removed a piece of candy, probably what was left of a Life Saver. After inspecting it a moment, he flipped it away and came into the yard. He didn't look at all surprised by what he saw. I was sure he had never seen anything like it before, but he had been around a long time, and he had seen many other strange things, so it was possible that nothing surprised him anymore. The deputy followed him into the yard, sticking as close as a small frightened child would stick to his father.

Mapes nodded, he didn't speak. I nodded back, but Candy didn't. Mapes stared at me with those ash-gray eyes another second; then he looked down at the spread. He nodded again. It was not to me this time; it was to his deputy. But the deputy was busy watching the old men with the shotguns.

"Griffin," Mapes said to him.

The deputy didn't answer.

"Griffin," Mapes said again.

Griffin turned from the old men to look at Mapes, but he seemed uncertain that Mapes had called his name.

"You said something, Sheriff?"

Mapes nodded toward the ground. Griffin glanced back over his shoulder toward the old men before leaning over and pulling back the spread. He quickly turned his head when he saw the bloody shirt, dirty face, dirty brown hair of Beau Boutan. Mapes didn't turn his head; he looked down at the body a good thirty seconds, and told Griffin to cover it up again. Griffin didn't hear him. He was busy watching the old men with the shotguns.

"Griffin," Mapes repeated.

Griffin glanced up at Mapes, but Mapes had already turned

away. Griffin covered up the body without looking at it.

"Go turn off that thing," Mapes said.

"Sir?" Griffin asked.

"The tractor, Griffin," Mapes said impatiently.

Griffin started toward the road.

"Griffin," Mapes called. His voice remained level, without inflection, yet meaningful.

"Yes, sir?" Griffin answered.

Mapes didn't turn around, so Griffin had to come back to face him.

"Get on that radio. Tell Russ—no one else—Russell to go back on that bayou and keep Fix there. No one else but him—and keep Fix and that crowd back there until he hears from me. And tell Herman to come out here and pick this up. But don't tell him who it is."

Griffin nodded, and started to leave again.

"Griffin," Mapes said, his voice still level.

Griffin stopped.

"First, turn off tractor," Mapes said. He was looking at Griffin as though Griffin were not very bright. "Second, call Russ. Third, call Herman. Tell him to come out here and pick up a *dead* body. No name. Fourth, can you remember all that between here and the car?"

"Of course, Sheriff."

Mapes stared down at Griffin until Griffin walked away. Then he turned his attention toward the old men with the guns.

"I counted seventeen, eighteen of them," he said. "Is that all of them?"

"I didn't count them," I said.

"And you?" he asked Candy. He did not look directly at her, he spoke to her from the side. Already he seemed to suspect that she had something to do with all these people being here.

"I don't know how many there are," she said. "But I can tell you what happened. I killed him."

Mapes looked down at her from over his left shoulder. He still suspected that she had gathered all these people here, but you could see he didn't believe that she had killed Beau Boutan.

"Over what?" he asked her.

"Beau Boutan still lived in the past," she said. "He still thought he could beat people like his paw did thirty, forty years ago. He started beating Charlie back there in the field, and Charlie ran up here to Mathu's house. I was standing there by the door talking to Mathu. We asked him what happened, and he said Beau hit him with a stalk of cane. A few minutes later Beau followed him on the tractor with the shotgun. When he stopped that tractor out there, I told him not to cross that ditch. I told him more than once, 'Beau, don't you cross that ditch.' Did he listen? You just don't beat people with a stalk of cane and hunt them like they're some kind of wild animal. You don't do that. I told him to stop, don't cross that ditch. I hollered at him not to cross that ditch. When he didn't stop, I reached and got that shotgun Mathu keeps beside the door. And I'll swear to that in court."

Mapes continued to look at her from the side. Once, while she was talking, he shot a quick glance at me. I could tell he didn't believe anything she was saying. Now she could see it, too.

"I'll swear to it in court," she said again. "And that's my story to the press."

Mapes grunted and turned to look at the people again. They had been watching and listening, but remained quiet. Even the children who sat on the steps were quiet but watching. The deputy came back into the yard and stood next to Mapes.

"Bring me one of them," Mapes said to him.

"Which one, Sheriff?" Griffin asked.

"One that can talk," Mapes said, without looking at Griffin.

Griffin left.

Candy had been standing a little behind Mapes, but now she moved in front to face him.

"I told you I did it," she said. "Why are you questioning them?"

Mapes didn't answer her.

"Candy, please," I said. I reached out to touch her, but she jerked her arm away from me.

"Because they're black and helpless, is that why you're picking on them?"

He ignored her. He was watching Griffin lead one of the old fellows toward him. The old man had to be eighty. Griffin was probably afraid of anyone younger. The old man wore overalls, a khaki shirt, and an old felt hat. He was a clean-shaven old fellow, walked with quick steps, leaning a bit forward. Candy moved to the side as Griffin led him up to Mapes. When Griffin released his arm, he took off his hat and held it to his chest. His head was shaved as clean as his face. He looked up at Mapes a second; then his eyes came down to Mapes's chest. He had a nervous twitch that made his bald head bob continually as if he were always agreeing with you. He was quite a bit shorter than Mapes, maybe even a foot shorter. Mapes let him stand there awhile before saying anything to him.

"How come you so far from home, Uncle Billy?" Mapes asked him.

"I kilt him," the old man said, without raising his eyes from Mapes's chest. His bald head never stopped bobbing.

"Now, I don't have time for that, Uncle Billy," Mapes said. "This is my fishing day. I ask you again, how come you so far from home?"

"I kilt—"

The back of Mapes's hand went *pow* across Uncle Billy's face, and spit shot from the old man's mouth as his head jerked to the side. Mapes had hit him so quickly that I hadn't seen it coming or expected it.

I heard a groan from the women sitting on the steps.

"Look at that, look at that," one of them said. "A old man like Billy Washington—just look at that."

"Mapes, I'm going to remember that," Candy said, stabbing her finger toward him. "I've got a lot of witnesses. I'm going to remember that."

Mapes paid her no attention.

"Let's try it again, Uncle Billy. How come you so far from home?"

"I kilt him," Uncle Billy said, his bald head bobbing.

Pow went Mapes's hand again. Blood dripped from Uncle Billy's mouth, but he would not wipe it away.

"Stand him over there, bring me another one," Mapes said to Griffin.

"You're going to beat them all, Mapes?" Candy asked him. She was mad enough to hit him, but Mapes probably would have hit her back. I didn't like what was going on either, but I knew that had I interfered, Mapes would have knocked hell out of me and thrown me in the back of his car.

"You better get her out of here," he said to me.

"Like hell he will," Candy said. "This is my land, in case you forget."

"You better stay out of my way," Mapes warned her.

"Like hell I will."

"Like hell you won't," he said.

He turned to the old man that Griffin had just brought up there.

"What are you doing from behind those trees, Gable?" he asked.

Gable was a thin, brown-skinned man with white hair and

high, prominent cheekbones. He was impeccably dressed—brown sports coat, plaid shirt, a string tie, brown trousers, and shoes well shined. He had taken off his hat, which he held against his leg, not to his chest as Uncle Billy had done. Also unlike Uncle Billy, who never raised his eyes higher than Mapes's chest, Gable looked him straight in the face.

"I kilt him," he said.

"I don't want to hurt you, Gable," Mapes said. "You've had enough trouble in your life already. Now, I ask you again, how did she get you from behind those trees?"

"I shot him," Gable said.

Mapes clamped his teeth so hard that the muscles in his heavy jowls began to quiver. His right hand came up slowly—then *pow*. Gable's face jerked to the side, but came right back. His eyes watered, but he stared Mapes straight in the face.

The women on the steps groaned. The little girl and the smaller boy covered their faces. The men watched quietly.

"You can do it all day long," Gable said to Mapes.

Mapes slapped him again. Gable's face jerked to the side just a little. His eyes blinked for a moment; then he was looking Mapes in the face again.

The muscles in Mapes's heavy jowls continued to quiver. He did not like what he was doing, but he didn't know any other way to get what he wanted.

"Stand him over there, bring me another one," he said.

"Not the other cheek?" Gable asked. "Both times you hit the same one—not the other one?"

Mapes's big face flushed with anger. The jowl muscles continued to twitch. He did not answer Gable.

Griffin took Gable by the arm and led him over to where Uncle Billy was standing. I saw Uncle Billy looking at Mapes and grinning. I could have told Mapes then that he wasn't going to get anywhere by slapping them.

"Why don't you use a stick or a hose pipe?" Candy said to

Mapes. "No sense bruising your hands on old people who can't fight back."

"They all have shotguns," Mapes said.

"You know they won't use them."

"That's right," Mapes said. "I know they won't use them, and we know they didn't use them, don't we?"

"I told you I did it," Candy said.

"Sure," Mapes said. "And my name is Santa Claus."

Griffin was moving among the crowd. Suddenly he had become very brave. He wasn't choosing the first one he came to; he was being picky now. He was going to get the one he wanted. The people did not look at him as he moved toward them. They didn't seem afraid; they just didn't think he was important enough to look at. But as he approached the steps, Aunt Glo's little grandson Snookum suddenly stood up before him. Griffin told him to sit back down before he slapped him down. Griffin was very tough around the very old and the very young. But instead of sitting back down, the boy jumped off the steps and started toward Mapes. Candy, who had not been standing too far away from Mapes, now got between him and the boy, and told the boy to go back. He stopped, but he did not return to the steps until his grandmother called him. He went back and sat on the steps next to her, and she put her arm around his shoulders. Then both she and he looked back at Mapes, and both seemed ready to be slapped, if either or both were his choice. Candy turned back to Mapes, but only stared at him, and did not say anything. I didn't say anything either. But I knew he wasn't going to get anything out of them by slapping them around.

Griffin had already chosen someone else, the quarter's preacher, Reverend Jameson. Griffin couldn't have chosen a sadder figure. His shirt was already fully wet from perspiration. He looked as if he were about to have a heart attack, he was so afraid of Mapes. Mapes didn't like it either that Griffin had brought him the preacher. He had wanted someone with a gun. But now he had no choice but to go on with what he had started.

"What are you doing down here, Reverend?" he asked. "Why aren't you at home reading your Bible?"

Reverend Jameson looked down at Mapes's feet. He did not raise his eyes as high as Mapes's chest.

"I ain't got nothing to say, Sheriff," he said, without raising his head.

"You better think of something to say," Mapes said. "What are you doing down here?"

Reverend Jameson shook his head, but never raised his eyes.

"I'll ask you one more time, Reverend," Mapes said. "What are you doing down here?"

The old man remained quiet. Beads of sweat covered his bald head. *Pow* went Mapes's hand across his face. Sweat flew from his bald head. Unlike the two other old men, whose faces snapped to the side when Mapes hit them, Reverend Jameson staggered and fell flat on his back. The people looked at him, but no one said anything. After a while he raised his head and looked at Candy the way a little dog would look up at its mistress after it has been punished. But Candy showed him no sympathy. None of the others did either. And he slowly pushed himself up and stood before Mapes again.

"Well?" Mapes said.

He shook his head, which was still bowed. "I ain't got nothing to say, Sheriff." And down he went again.

He sat up just as he had done before, and stared down at the ground. Then, as he started pushing himself to his feet, suddenly every last person in the yard and on the porch, whether he was sitting, squatting, or standing, began forming a line up to Mapes. Candy was at the head of the line.

"I'm next, Mapes," she said.

Mapes stared at her with those hard, ash-colored eyes, and

his flushed heavy jowls trembled even more violently. I thought he was going to hit her for sure now, and I was just about ready to step between them when he jerked his head and walked away, and I knew he wanted me to follow him out into the road. He leaned back against his car and crossed his legs and folded his arms across his chest. He was a big man—two sixty, two seventy—and he looked very tired. I leaned back against the car beside him, and both of us looked into the yard. The people had begun moving around again. Candy was attending to Uncle Billy, wiping his mouth with a handkerchief. And I noticed for the first time that the only person who had not gotten into the line was Mathu. He still squatted against the wall with the gun cradled in his arms. He was smoking a cigarette and looking out at us.

"You know he did it, don't you?" Mapes said. He had calmed down some.

"Who?" I said.

"You know who I'm talking about."

Yes, I knew who he was talking about. We were both looking at him squatting there.

"Why don't you arrest him?" I said.

"On what charges?" Mapes asked.

"Killing Beau, I suppose."

"How can you prove it?" Mapes said. "Because Beau was killed here in his yard? That's no proof. Clinton would have that thrown out of court in two seconds flat. And she knows that, too."

"What about the gun?"

"You didn't look very close, did you?" Mapes asked me. "Every last one has the same make gun—twelve-gauge. Everyone probably has the same numbered shell in the gun right now. No, you can't arrest him on that. But he killed him, all right. The only one with nuts enough to do it."

He got a half roll of Life Savers out of his pocket and

reached it toward me. I shook my head. He put one of the Life Savers into his mouth, and the pack back into his pocket. He sucked on the Life Saver while he looked at Mathu squatting against the wall.

"You seen Charlie?" he asked me.

"No, I haven't seen him."

"He's probably hiding somewhere back there in the field," Mapes said. "We can pick him up anytime. But he didn't do it. Mathu did. And *she* arranged this little get-together. Not him. He never would have. He's a tough old goat just like you see him there. He probably would have turned himself in by now if she hadn't got into it, but he doesn't want to go against her. Where she got all these old men from, only God knows. Look at them. Look at those old guns."

We both looked at the old men with their shotguns. Candy had finished attending to Uncle Billy and Gable, and she had gone back to the steps to stand beside Aunt Glo and the children. She and Aunt Glo were talking and looking out into the road at us.

"My God, man, can't you talk to her?" Mapes said to me. "I don't want any trouble on this place. That Baton Rouge crowd's already getting drunk for that game tomorrow. Some of them wouldn't want anything better than a necktie party tonight."

"I tried talking. She wouldn't listen," I said.

"You tried throwing her butt into the back of that car?" Mapes asked.

"No, I didn't try that, Mapes," I told him. "I hear there's a law against kidnapping people. Especially on their own place."

"There's a law against harboring a murderer, too," Mapes said. "You ever heard of that law?"

I didn't answer him. I looked at Candy standing beside the steps talking to Aunt Glo.

"You two are going to make a hell of a marriage," Mapes said.

"Don't get personal, Mapes," I told him.

"When is the date?" he asked, and grinned.

"Just don't get personal, all right, Mapes?"

He exhaled a deep breath while he looked at me. I wasn't much of a man in his eyesight. He looked back at Candy.

"Maybe Beau was living in the past, and maybe he wasn't, but she damned sure is," he said. "She still thinks she can do as her paw and the rest of them did fifty years ago. Well, it's not going to work. He isn't getting out of this."

"You seem to have something personal against him."

Mapes grunted. "That's where you're wrong. I admire the nigger. He's a better man than most I've met, black or white. But he killed a man—and she's not getting him out of it. If she had any sense at all, she would have taken him to jail hours ago. Because if Fix doesn't show up, others may. And they won't be coming here to talk. But I don't suppose she realizes that."

He looked at me to see if I had any comments. I had nothing to say. He looked past me. "Well, here comes Herman," he said.

The hearse drove slowly down the road. It went by us, then stopped in front of Mapes's car, and the coroner and his assistant remained inside awhile looking out at the people. The people in the yard and on the porch looked back at the hearse.

The coroner got out and looked at the people again before coming toward Mapes. He was a small, clean-shaven man with steel-rim glasses. He could have been in his mid- or late sixties. He wore a seersucker suit, a panama hat, a white shirt, and a small polka-dotted bow tie. His well-shined black shoes were covered with dust.

"Herman," Mapes said.

But Herman did not speak. Instead, he just looked up at

Mapes, and I could see his blue eyes through the thick lenses asking Mapes what it was all about. Mapes moved the Life Saver around with his tongue and nodded to the assistant, who had followed the coroner over to us. The assistant, who was named George, was a much younger and larger man. He was blond and balding.

"George," Mapes said.

"Mapes," George said.

Then George started looking at Mapes exactly the way that Herman was doing. They wanted Mapes to say something to them. They thought Mapes owed them some kind of explanation about what was going on. Mapes didn't say anything. He looked into the yard where all the people were looking out at us. He moved the Life Saver around before turning back to Herman. Old Herman was still looking up at him.

"Don't you think you ought to get started?" Mapes said.

Herman waited about ten more seconds before he said, "Sure, Mapes." Then he looked up at Mapes another ten seconds before he said anything to George. "Bring that stretcher and a blanket," he said. Then, while George was getting the stretcher and blanket out of the hearse, Herman looked up at Mapes another ten or fifteen seconds before going into the yard. After a while, Mapes and I followed him.

"How long you reckon he's been dead?" Mapes asked.

Herman was on one knee looking down at Beau.

"Two, maybe three hours, I suppose," he said.

"More like three," Mapes said. "That would put it around noon, wouldn't it?"

"Around that time, I suppose," Herman said.

"I been here half an hour," Mapes said. "Got here around two-thirty. That would have given them—her—a two-and-a-half-hour jump—"

"What?" Herman said.

"Just talking to myself," Mapes said.

Herman couldn't hold back any longer, and jumped to his feet. For an old man he could really get up fast. He got up right against Mapes's chest. He was about half the size of Mapes.

"What the hell is going on around here, Mapes?" he said, pushing up against Mapes's stomach. "You're talking to yourself while a bunch of niggers stand around here with shotguns and a white man lays dead in the grass. I demand to know what the hell is going on around here!"

"You and George better get him into Bayonne," Mapes said calmly.

George was standing there with the stretcher and the blanket. Herman was still staring at Mapes through those thick lenses which made his eyes look about the size of partridge eggs. You could not pass your hand slantwise between Herman's chest and Mapes's stomach.

"I don't know any more than you do," Mapes said, looking over Herman down at the corpse.

"Don't you think you ought to hurry up and find out more than I know?" Herman asked, still looking up at Mapes.

"You take care your business, I'll take care mine," Mapes said.

"Sure," the coroner said, and nodded. He turned to his assistant. "All right, George."

George spread the blanket out on the grass, and he and Griffin picked up Beau by the arms and legs and laid him on the blanket. Then George wrapped the blanket well around and over Beau, and he and Griffin laid Beau on the stretcher and took him out to the hearse. Everyone in the yard and on the porch watched what was going on, but remained quiet.

"Don't you think you ought to hurry, Mapes?" Herman asked him one more time. "Not only Fix—but what about his friends on the *lane?*" Behind the thick lenses his blue eyes got even bigger when he mentioned the friends on the lane. The eyes, not the words, gave the meaning of what he had just said.

"Don't spread this around," Mapes said, and moved the candy about in his mouth.

The coroner shook his head. "Oh, no, Mapes," he said. "I won't tell a soul. I'll just tell them Beau has a chill in all this hot weather—that's why I got him wrapped up like this."

"The rest of it, I mean," Mapes said.

"The shotguns?"

"Exactly."

"Don't worry," the coroner said. "Nobody would believe me anyhow. Would you, Mapes?"

Mapes didn't answer him. The coroner looked around at the people, then back at Mapes again. But he could see that Mapes had no more to say to him, and after looking up at me helplessly he left the yard. George was already in the hearse waiting for him. After they had driven off, Mapes took off his hat and wiped the sweatband. He wiped his face and neck while he looked at the people on the porch.

"All right," he said when he had put the hat back on. "The ones who don't stay here get moving. The rest of you move back there on the porch. I mean right now."

But nobody moved.

"What's the matter with you all?" Mapes asked them. "Can't you all hear, either? I said move."

"I kilt him," Uncle Billy said. Uncle Billy stood by the garden fence where Griffin had put him half an hour ago. His lips were swollen from where Mapes had hit him. He seemed as proud of his swollen lips as was Crane's boy in *The Red Badge of Courage*.

Mapes stared at him a second, then went toward him. Everyone expected Mapes to pop him again. Instead, he jerked the gun out of Uncle Billy's hand, ejected the shell, and raised it to his nose. Then he put the shell back, and slammed the gun into the waiting hands.

"Who told you to fire that gun, Uncle Billy?" Mapes asked him.

"Nobody," Uncle Billy said.

"Candy, didn't she?" Mapes asked.

"No, sir," Uncle Billy said.

"You still go to church, Uncle Billy?" Mapes asked him.

"A deacon at Little Shadrack Baptist Church," Uncle Billy said.

"If I got a Bible, would you still say you shot Beau, Uncle Billy?"

Uncle Billy licked his bottom lip, and he lowered his head as though he had to give this great consideration. Mapes waited. We all waited. Mapes got tired waiting.

"Well?" he said.

Uncle Billy raised his head and, looking Mapes straight in the eyes, he nodded.

"You didn't shoot Beau, now, did you, Uncle Billy?" Mapes asked him again.

"Yes, sir, Sheriff."

"Candy put you up to all this, now, didn't she?" Mapes asked the old man. "Don't worry, I won't let her do you anything. I promise you."

"No, sir, I did it all on my own," Uncle Billy said, his head continually bobbing.

"Was Candy down here when you got here?" Mapes asked, using a different tactic now.

"I don't rightly know," Uncle Billy said.

"What you mean you don't rightly know?" Mapes asked. "That's her car out there. Was her car here?"

"I can't rightly tell," the old man said.

"You mean you can't rightly see—that's what you mean, don't you, Uncle Billy?"

"Oh, I sees pretty well, Sheriff, pretty well indeed."

Mapes looked at the old man with exasperation. He was getting awfully tired.

"When did you hear about the killing, Uncle Billy? One o'clock?"

"I didn't have to hear about it, Sheriff. I was right here. I did it."

"What were you doing when Candy called you? Taking a nap? Eating dinner? What, Uncle Billy?"

"Didn't call me at all," Uncle Billy said. "I was right here. And I shot him."

Mapes's big face had turned redder with exasperation. He wanted to hit the old man again, maybe even choke him.

"You ever seen anybody die in the electric chair, old man?" Mapes asked Uncle Billy.

Uncle Billy's head went on bobbing. "No, sir," he said.

"It's not a pretty sight, Uncle Billy. Not when that juice hit you. That's how you want to go?"

"No, sir. But if I have to."

"Even if you have to, Uncle Billy, you don't want to go that way," Mapes told him. "When that juice hit you, I've seen that chair dance. You see, Uncle Billy, we don't have a permanent chair in Bayonne. When we need one, we go to Angola to pick it up. And we don't waste time screwing it down—not for just one killing. And when that juice hit you, I've seen that chair rattle, I've seen it dance. Not a pretty sight, old man. Is that how you want to go?"

"No, sir."

"Then what you think'll happen if I took you in and they convicted you? You think you're too old to die in the chair?"

"No, sir."

"Well?"

The old man licked his swollen bottom lip and looked down at the ground again. I thought Mapes had finally got to him. Everybody on the porch and in the yard was watching and waiting.

"I don't have all day, Uncle Billy," Mapes said.

The old man started shaking his head as he looked up at Mapes again.

"I kilt him," he said.

"Why?" Mapes asked him.

"Sir?"

"Why did you kill Beau?"

"What they did my boy," the old man said, staring blankly at Mapes, his head bobbing again. His swollen bottom lip trembled nervously. "The way they beat him. They beat him till they beat him crazy, and we had to send him to Jackson. He don't even know me and his mama no more. We take him candy, we take him cake, he eat it like a hog eating corn. Don't offer none to them other crazy people. Don't offer none to nobody—me, his mama, or them other crazy people. Just put his head in the cake and eat it like a hog eating corn. His mama slice him a little piece and hand it to him, he let it fall on the table, and eat it like a hog eating corn. That's no way to be. It hurt his mama every time she sees that."

"Who beat your boy, Uncle Billy?" Mapes asked the old man.

"Fix and them, what the people say."

"But you don't know for sure?"

"I can just take what the people say. I wasn't there."

"When did all this happen, Uncle Billy?"

"Years back, when he come home from that war."

"What war?"

"That war with Hitler and them Japs."

"You've been holding a grudge against Fix all that time, Uncle Billy?"

"I don't hold no grudge. My Bible tells me not to hold no grudge."

"Your Bible also tells you thou shalt not kill."

"Yes, sir. It does."

"Well?"

"Sometimes you just has to go against your Bible, Sheriff," Uncle Billy told Mapes. His bald head didn't stop bobbing.

"You didn't," Mapes said. "I don't think you even know who shot Beau. You're just a pawn. Somebody they're playing with. You weren't even down here, and they didn't even tell you who did it, or how it happened—now, did they?"

"No, sir. They didn't need to tell me. I did it."

Mapes looked around the yard, then back at the old man again.

"Aim at one of the bean poles in that garden, Uncle Billy," Mapes said.

"What one?" the old man asked.

"What one you can see," Mapes told him.

"I sees a bunch of them," the old man said, his bald head steadily bobbing.

"Aim," Mapes commanded, with exasperation.

Uncle Billy set the gun against his shoulder and aimed at the nearest pole about ten feet away. For a moment, he didn't even know which eye to shut. When he finally figured that out, the gun was shaking so much you would have thought it was one of those divining rods that had just discovered water.

"You can bring it down," Mapes said. The old man lowered the gun. He was sweating he was so tired. "It would have taken Beau longer than that to stop that tractor, get his gun, and come into this yard," Mapes said. "You're still saying you killed him."

"I didn't sight till he crossed that ditch," Uncle Billy said.

"The one who shot Beau, his hands didn't tremble, Uncle Billy," Mapes said. "He was cool about it, cool and calm. Knew exactly what he was doing. Shot at the right moment, the right distance. A hunter shot Beau, Uncle Billy. Somebody used to guns. Not you. You never hunted a thing in your life but a good seat in a Baptist church. In winter, near the heater—in summer, near the window. Get out of my sight, Uncle Billy. Go stand somewhere else."

"Yes, sir," the old man said. "But I did it."

"I told you to move," Mapes said.

"Yes, sir, I'm moving," he said, backing away, his head bobbing all the time. "But I did it."

"Now, what would I look like taking something like that to Bayonne?" Mapes was talking to himself again. "They'd laugh me out of the parish, if they don't lock me in the loony ward and throw away the key first." He turned his head slowly and looked at Mathu squatting against the wall. "Mathu, come down here," he said.

Joseph Seaberry

aka

Rufe

———

When Mapes called Mathu, Candy moved between Mapes and the steps. The rest of us came in a little bit closer, too. Mapes looked around at the people closing in on him, but he wasn't worried, and he looked back at Mathu. Mathu had stood up with his gun, and he was headed toward the steps.

"Stay where you're at," Candy said.

"I'll come to the man," Mathu said.

"Just one second," Candy said. "I mean it." She looked at him till he stopped; then she turned back to Mapes. "Mind, Mapes," she said. "Mind your hands, now. He's not Reverend Jameson. He's not Uncle Billy or Gable. Mind your hands, now."

"He's Mathu," Mapes said. "But I represent the law. And I did find a dead man in his yard. That gives me the right to question even Mathu."

"You just mind your hands," Candy warned him. "One drop of his blood—" She stopped. She didn't have to say the rest.

"I think he know what you mean, Candy," Clatoo said, from the end of the garry.

"Yes, I think he does," Candy said, still looking at Mapes.

Then she reached out her hand to help Mathu down the steps. Two of the four steps was missen, had been missen twenty, twenty-five years, and Mathu had come down them steps every day of his life without anybody helping him. But since Candy reached out her hand, he took it just to please her.

When he reached the ground, he bowed to thank her; then he turned to Mapes. He was up in his eighties, head white as it could be, but you didn't see no trembling in his face, in his hands. He faced Mapes straight and tall, holding his gun close to his side.

"How you feeling, Mathu?" Mapes asked.

Mapes was a lot of things. He was big, mean, brutal. But Mapes respected a man. Mathu was a man, and Mapes respected Mathu. But he didn't think much of the rest of us, and he didn't respect us.

"I'm all right, Sheriff," Mathu said. "And yourself?"

"I'm tired," Mapes said. "I had thought I'd get a little fishing in today."

"They biting good, what I hear," Mathu said. His head up, he was looking straight at Mapes. He wasn't quite as tall as Mapes. Built like a picket—no, more like a post. A old post in the ground—narrow but still strong, and not leaning, and not trembling, either.

Mapes looked at him. Mapes liked Mathu. They had hunted together. Wildcats, alligators, deers. They had fished together. And Mapes had had a few drinks with Mathu at Mathu's house. He liked Mathu. Even when Mathu got into trouble and he had to arrest Mathu, he knowed it wasn't Mathu's doing. But he knowed Mathu had never backed down from anybody, either. Maybe that's why he liked him. To him Mathu was a real man. The rest of us wasn't.

"Tell them to go home, Mathu," Mapes said.

"That's up to them, Sheriff."

"They'll do it if you tell them to do it," Mapes said. "Tell them to go home before there's trouble."

"Mathu, you don't have to answer any questions," Candy said. She hadn't left his side since he stepped to the ground. "He can take you to jail if he wants to, but he can't force you to talk. Not until Clinton gets there."

"I don't mind talking," Mathu said.

"Tell them to tell me who did it, Mathu," Mapes said. He looked at Mathu, never at Candy. He was still being respectful toward Mathu.

"I did it, Sheriff," Mathu said.

Mapes nodded. "I know you did it," he said. "You're the only one around here man enough. But I have to hear it from one of them. One of them must say he was called here after it happened."

"I can't make nobody say what they don't want to say," Mathu said.

"Do you want to see any of these people hurt, Mathu?"

"No, Sheriff."

"You know that can happen now, don't you?" Mapes asked him. Mapes was reminding him of Fix, but not using Fix's name. His eyes was saying Fix, not his mouth.

"A man got to do what he think is right, Sheriff," Mathu said. "That's what part him from a boy."

"It's not a matter of right and wrong, Mathu," Mapes said. "It's a matter of a lot of people getting hurt. And you know you don't want that."

"No, I don't. But it's up to them."

"It's up to you, Mathu," Mapes said. "Only you. And I ask you, man to man, tell them to go home."

Mathu started looking round. I don't know what he was going to say, but he didn't get a chance to say it, anyhow.

"It ain't go'n work this time, Sheriff," Clatoo said, from the end of the garry.

Mapes turned his head quick. "Who said that?" he asked. He heard where the voice came from, and he knowed it was Clatoo's voice, but he didn't think Clatoo would own up to it. "I said who said that?" he asked.

"I did, Sheriff," Clatoo said.

Mapes pretended he couldn't find Clatoo in the crowd. Clatoo was the only person sitting on that end of the garry, and still Mapes pretended he couldn't find him. Then when he did, he stared at Clatoo long and hard. He thought if he stared at him long enough, Clatoo was bound to look down. But Clatoo didn't look down. He sat there with that shotgun over his legs, looking straight back at Mapes.

"What's the matter with you, Clatoo?" Mapes said. "You're the last person I thought would be looking for trouble."

"That's been my trouble," Clatoo said.

"What?" Mapes said. Mapes was looking at him the way white folks do round here, looking at him hard.

"I ain't had no trouble with the law," Clatoo said.

"Meaning?" Mapes said.

"I'm old," Clatoo said.

"Meaning?" Mapes said.

"About time I had li'l trouble with the law before I died," Clatoo said.

"You really want to go to jail, don't you?" Mapes said.

"I figured I was on my way there when I shot him," Clatoo said.

"Amen," Beulah said, from the steps.

Mapes looked at Clatoo the way white folks know how to look at a nigger when they think he's being smart.

"Isn't it a little bit late for you to be getting militant around here?" Mapes asked Clatoo.

"I always been militant," Clatoo said. "My intrance gone sour, keeping my militance down."

"Sure now," Mapes said, looking at him hard.

"Sure now is right," Clatoo said. "No use talking to Mathu. He didn't do nothing. I did it."

"Sure now," Mapes said.

"Now, there y'all go again, there y'all go again," Dirty Red said. Dirty Red was squatting by the walk with that little short, wet cigarette hanging from the corner of his mouth. If it was not the same one he had a minute ago, it looked just like it. You never seen Dirty Red lighting a new cigarette. When you seen it, it was already half gone—wet, dirty-looking, and half gone. He probably had a bunch of them in his pocket like that—dirty and half gone. "I don't see how come y'all won't let a man get—"

"Shut up," Mapes said. "You and nobody in your family ever done a thing in this world but worked hard to avoid work."

"Till today," Dirty Red said. He looked up at Mapes, with his head cocked a little to the side to keep the smoke out his eyes. "Today, I—"

"You trying to cut in on me when I'm talking to you?" Mapes asked him.

"Look like he's doing more than just trying," Johnny Paul said, from the other side of Mapes.

Mapes turned quick. Just his head. He was too fat to turn his body fast. "You, too, Johnny Paul?" he said.

Johnny Paul nodded his head. "Me too."

Mapes was still looking around at Johnny Paul when Jacob Aguillard spoke up.

"No, Dirty Red, Johnny Paul. Uh-uh, Clatoo. It was me," he said. "I remember what that crowd did to my sister."

"I see," Mapes said, looking at Jacob now.

"You see what?" Johnny Paul said.

Mapes was still looking at Jacob when Ding Lejeune spoke up. Ding and his brother Bing stood close together between the walk and the garden.

"I kilt him," Ding said, thumping his chest. "Me, me—not them, not my brother. Me. What they did to my sister's little girl—Michelle Gigi."

"I see," Mapes said, looking at Ding and Bing at the same time. "I see."

Johnny Paul grunted out loud. "No, you don't see."

He wasn't looking at Mapes, he was looking toward the tractor and the trailers of cane out there in the road. But I could tell he wasn't seeing any of that. I couldn't tell what he was thinking until I saw his eyes shifting up the quarters where his mama and papa used to stay. But the old house wasn't there now. It had gone like all the others had gone. Now weeds covered the place where the house used to be. "Y'all look," he said. "Look now. Y'all see anything? What y'all see?"

"I see nothing but weeds, Johnny Paul," Mapes said. "If that's what you're trying to say."

"Yes, sir," Johnny Paul said. He didn't look at Mapes; he was still looking up the quarters. "Yes, sir, I figured that's all you would see. But what do the rest don't see? What y'all don't see, Rufe?" he asked me. He didn't look at me, still looking up the quarters. "What y'all don't see, Clatoo? What y'all don't see, Glo? What y'all don't see, Corrine, Rooster, Beulah? What y'all don't see, all the rest of y'all?"

"I don't have time for people telling me what they can't or don't see, Johnny Paul," Mapes said. "I want—"

Johnny Paul turned on him. He was tall as Mapes, but thin, thin. He was the color of Brown Mule chewing tobacco. His eyes gray, gray like Mapes's eyes, but not hard like Mapes's eyes. He looked dead at Mapes.

"You ain't got nothing but time, Sheriff."

"What?" Mapes said.

"I did it," Johnny Paul said.

"I see," Mapes said. "Either I stand here and let you talk about things you don't see, and the things the others don't see, or I take you in? I see."

"Yes, sir," Johnny Paul said. "But you still don't see. Yes, sir, what you see is the weeds, but you don't see what we don't see."

"Do you see it, Johnny Paul?" Mapes asked him.

"No, I don't see it," Johnny Paul said. "That's why I kilt him."

"I see," Mapes said.

"No, you don't," Johnny Paul said. "No, you don't. You had to be here to don't see it now. You just can't come down here every now and then. You had to live here seventy-seven years to don't see it now. No, Sheriff, you don't see. You don't even know what I don't see."

"Do you know what you don't see?" Mapes asked him.

"Ask Mathu," Johnny Paul said.

"No, I'm asking you," Mapes said. "I'll get back to Mathu later."

"Ask Glo," Johnny Paul said. "Ask Tucker. Gable. Clatoo. Ask Yank. Jameson there. Ask any of them, all of them what they don't see no more."

"All right," Mapes said. "Tell me. But make it quick. I can still get in some fishing."

"You still don't see," Johnny Paul said. "You still don't see. I don't have to make nothing quick. I can take all the time in the world I want, and it ain't nothing you can do but take me to jail. You can't slap me hard enough to hurt me no more, Sheriff."

"I see," Mapes said.

Johnny Paul kicked the ground. Thin as he was and kicking the ground like that coulda fractured his leg.

"Do you?" he said. "Do you? Do you hear that church bell ringing?"

"Are you all right?" Mapes asked him. "And maybe I shoulda asked you that before. Maybe I shoulda asked all y'all that before," he said, looking at the rest of us. Then back to Johnny Paul. "Church bells, Johnny Paul?"

"I hear him," Beulah said from the steps. "He's making sense."

"Then tell me in English what he's saying in Gri-gri," Mapes said.

"Let him tell you," Beulah said. "He talks good as I do."

"You want to go too, huh?" Mapes asked her.

"That's right," Beulah said. "I don't mind going. I been to the pen before. You was saying, Johnny Paul?"

"Y'all remember how it used to be?" Johnny Paul said. He wasn't answering Beulah, he wasn't even speaking to her, or to Mapes now. He was just thinking out loud, the way a man talk to himself plowing the field by himself or hunting in the swamps with nothing but a gun, not even a dog. "Remember?" he said. "When they wasn't no weeds—remember? Remember how they used to sit out there on the garry—Mama, Papa, Aunt Clara, Aunt Sarah, Unc Moon, Aunt Spoodle, Aunt Thread. Remember? Everybody had flowers in the yard. But nobody had four-o'clocks like Jack Toussaint. Every day at four o'clock, they opened up just as pretty. Remember?" He stopped, thinking back. The rest of us all thinking back. I had spent many, many days on the end of Jack's garry, facing that bush. But you wouldn't never catch it opening. It opened while you was sitting there, but you never saw it. Like trying to watch a hour hand move on a clock. You never see it move, but it was moving all the time.

"That's why I kilt him, that's why," Johnny Paul said. "To protect them little flowers. But they ain't here no more. And how come? 'Cause Jack ain't here no more. He's back there under them trees with all the rest. With Mama and Papa, Aunt Thread, Aunt Spoodle, Aunt Clara, Unc Moon, Unc Jerry—all the rest of them. But y'all do remember, don't y'all?" He turned to Glo. Glo sat there on the steps, still wearing her apron, her little grandchildren at her side. She was looking down at the ground, remembering. She nodded. "Remember the palm-of-Christians in Thread's yard, Glo? Other people had them, but they didn't grow nowhere thick and dark like they did in her yard. Remember, Glo?" Glo nodded again, not looking at him. She was seeing the palm-of-Christians. I was seeing the palm-of-Christians. That's when you was a little boy, you used to drag a little girl under them leaves. It was the coolest place in summer. If it was raining, storming, the leaves was so big, they kept the water off you. "Remember Jack and Red Rider hitting that field every morning with them two mules, Diamond and Job?" Johnny Paul asked us. He wasn't looking at Glo now; he was looking way off again. "Lord, Lord, Lord. Don't tell me you can't remember them early mornings when that sun was just coming up over there behind them trees? Y'all can't tell me y'all can't remember how Jack and Red Rider used to race out into that field on them old single slides? Jack with Diamond, Red Rider with Job—touching the ground, just touching the ground to keep them slides steady. Hah. Tell me who could beat them two men plowing a row, hanh? Who? I'm asking y'all who?"

"Nobody," Beulah said. "That's for sure. Not them two men. Them was men—them."

Johnny Paul nodded his head. Not to Beulah. He wasn't looking at her. He was looking way off again, down the quarters toward the field.

"Thirty, forty of us going out in the field with cane knives, hoes, plows—name it. Sunup to sundown, hard, miserable work, but we managed to get it done. We stuck together, shared what little we had, and loved and respected each other.

"But just look at things today. Where the people? Where the roses? Where the four-o'clocks? The palm-of-Christians? Where the people used to sing and pray in the church? I'll tell you. Under them trees back there, that's where. And where they used to stay, the weeds got it now, just waiting for the tractor to come plow it up."

Johnny Paul had been looking down the quarters. He looked at Mapes again. The people had been nodding their heads, going along with him all the time.

"That's something you can't see, Sheriff, 'cause you never could see it," he said. "You can't see Red Rider with Job, Jack with Diamond. You can't see the church with the people, and you can't hear the singing and the praying. You had to be here then to be able to don't see it and don't hear it now. But I was here then, and I don't see it now, and that's why I did it. I did it for them back there under them trees. I did it 'cause that tractor is getting closer and closer to that graveyard, and I was scared if I didn't do it, one day that tractor was go'n come in there and plow up them graves, getting rid of all proof that we ever was. Like now they trying to get rid of all proof that black people ever farmed this land with plows and mules—like if they had nothing from the starten but motor machines. Sure, one day they will get rid of the proof that we ever was, but they ain't go'n do it while I'm still here. Mama and Papa worked too hard in these fields. They mama and they papa worked too hard in these same fields. They mama and they papa people worked too hard, too hard to have that tractor just come in that graveyard and destroy all proof that they ever was. I'm the last one left. I had to see that the graves stayed for a little while longer. But I just didn't do it for my own people. I did it for every last one back there under them trees. And I did it for every four-o'clock, every rosebush, every palm-of-Christian ever growed on this place."

He went over to the garden fence to stand by himself. The people stayed quiet. Even Mapes was quiet. Mathu was still there before Mapes, Candy not too far from Mathu, and her boyfriend, Lou, not too far from her side.

Mapes grunted. Not loud. Quiet. He was starting to feel what was going on. If he felt it right, he knowed he had to wait. He kept the Life Saver quiet, waiting. Then Tucker spoke up. And Mapes started moving the candy around in his mouth again.

Tucker was a small, brown-skinned fellow. I hadn't seen Tucker in—Lord, let me see—say, maybe two, three years. Last time was at Edna Zeno's funeral down the road at Little Zion. He used to live here, him and his family, twenty-five, thirty years ago, but most of his people was dead now, and he lived at Jarreau, about eight miles from here, going toward Bayonne.

"Y'all remember my brother Silas, don't y'all?" he said. "I'm talking to the old, not to the young. You don't remember him, Candy. They got rid of him 'fore you was born. He was the last black man round here trying to sharecrop on this place. The last one to fight against that tractor out there."

Some of us looked at the tractor and the two loads of cane. Mapes didn't; he was looking down at the ground. He was getting tired; he was getting tired fast. Tired listening, tired standing, tired of niggers. But he didn't know what to do about it. He could take Mathu to jail, but what about the rest of us—specially Candy? So now he was just looking down at the ground, thinking. He had already used his only little knowledge he knowed how to deal with black folks—knocking them around. When that didn't change a thing, when people started getting in line to be knocked around, he didn't know what else to do. So now he just stood there, a big fat red hulk, looking down at the ground.

"We told him to stop," Tucker was saying. "We all told

him the rest of us had gived up, and he ought to give up, too—we all told him that. We tried to show him how it couldn't work. We had got the worst land from the start, and no matter how hard we worked it, the people with the best land was go'n always be in front. All you old people know this already. After the plantation was dying out, the Marshalls dosed out the land for sharecropping, giving the best land to the Cajuns, and giving us the worst—that bottomland near the swamps. Here, our own black people had been working this land a hundred years for the Marshall plantation, but when it come to sharecropping, now they give the best land to the Cajuns, who had never set foot on the land before."

He stopped and looked at Candy. Candy was standing by Mathu, her mouth tight, grim—she was looking over the yard, down the quarters, toward the fields. She knowed Tucker was telling the truth. She hadn't witnessed it, she was born too late to witness it, but she had heard about what had happened. She had heard about it from Mathu, from the rest of us—and she knowed he was telling the truth.

"I'm stating facts," Tucker said. "Facts. 'Cause this is the day of reckonding, and I will speak the truth, without fear, if it mean I have to spend the rest of my life in jail."

Mapes grunted—a grunt that said you might.

"Yeah, you can go on and grunt all you want," Tucker said to Mapes. "But all you can do is lock me up. Here, you want lock me up?" he said, coming on Mapes with his hands out. "Here, I'm ready. Go on and lock me up."

Mapes just looked at him, and moved that candy around in his mouth.

"I wish I was the sheriff round here," the deputy said. All this time, he had been standing to the side, looking mad, but staying quiet. "I bet you wouldn't be talking to me like that."

"And what would you do, you little no-butt nothing?" Tucker said to the little deputy.

The people laughed. That little deputy turned red.

"Shut up," Mapes said to him.

"I ain't used to no niggers talking to me like that," the deputy said.

"Just stick around long enough," Beulah said, from the steps.

"We go'n just stand here and take this?" the deputy asked Mapes.

"You can go for a walk," Mapes said. "I'll call you if I need you."

"I don't feel like walking," the deputy said. "Left just to me, that old coon woulda been in jail an hour ago. And I'd shoot the first one tried to get him loose." He looked at Candy.

Candy stared at him from over by the steps. She looked at him slow and hard, that Marshall way of looking at you. The little deputy stood his ground for a while, but when he saw Candy wasn't going to back down, he turned from her and looked back at Tucker again. Now he was trying to make Tucker look down.

"Take a walk," Mapes said.

"I don't feel like walking," the deputy said.

"Then just be quiet," Mapes said. "Let them work out their gall. You was saying?" he said to Tucker.

"That boy through?" Tucker asked Mapes.

"He's through," Mapes said.

"You through, boy?" Tucker asked the deputy himself.

That little deputy didn't answer. He just looked at Tucker. Tucker looked right back at him.

"Y'all know what happened," Tucker said. He wasn't looking at Mapes; he was still looking at that little deputy. But after a while he didn't think that little deputy was worth looking at, and he turned to us. "Y'all remember how he drove his wife and children, trying to keep up with the machine. Drove her till he drove her crazy. But even that didn't stop him. He wouldn't stop till one day they caught him and beat him in the ground."

He stopped—not looking at us now—looking away. We all stayed quiet. Everything was quiet—the weeds, the fields, the swamps—everything quiet, quiet. Waiting for him to go on.

"Y'all don't know 'cause y'all wasn't there, and I ain't been able to talk about it before," he said. He turned to us again. "Been in here all these years, boiling in me," he said, hitting his chest. "Done spoiled my intrance. Fear. Fear. Done spoiled my intrance. I don't know how come I'm still alive."

He turned to Glo. Glo nodded her head. She knowed what he was talking about. We all knowed what he was talking about.

"How can a man beat a machine?" he asked. "No way? Hanh? That's what you say? Well, my brother did. With them two little mules, he beat that tractor to the derrick. Them two little mules did all they could, like my brother did. They knowed it was the end if they couldn't make it. They could hear the machine like everybody else could hear the machine, and they knowed they had to pull, pull, pull if they wanted to keep going. My brother and mules, mules and my brother. So they pulled for him and pulled for him and pulled for him, sweating, slipping, falling, but pulling for him. Slobber running from their mouths, the bit cutting their lips, the slobber and blood mixing and falling to the ground, yet they pulled, pulled, pulled in all that mud for him. And yes, they did win. They won. But they wasn't supposed to win. How can flesh and blood and nigger win against white man and machine?

"So they beat him. They took stalks of cane and they beat him and beat him and beat him. I was there, and I didn't move. I was loading cane for Tony O'linde, me and Joe Taylor. I saw the race, I saw my brother beat Felix Boutan on his tractor. I wouldn't be lying this day for nothing in the world. I saw my brother win that race. But he wasn't supposed to win, he was supposed to lose. We all knowed he was supposed to lose. Me, his own brother, knowed he was supposed to lose. He was supposed to lose years ago, and because he didn't lose like a nigger is supposed to lose, they beat him. And they beat him, and they beat him. And I didn't do nothing but stand there and watch them beat my brother down to the ground."

He stopped again. He looked at all of us. But none of us looked back at him. We had all done the same thing some-time or another; we had all seen our brother, sister, mama, daddy insulted once and didn't do a thing about it.

Tucker had been standing near the steps all the time he was talking. Now he went to the far end of the garry and looked toward the graveyard. You couldn't see a thing from here for the weeds. But we all knowed where his eyes was; we all knowed who he was talking to. All of us had stood here—in one of these old yards—and we had all hollered toward that graveyard.

"Forgive me!" He had both hands over his head, the gun in one hand, the other hand clenched to a fist. "Forgive this nothing!" he called. "Can you hear me, Silas? Tell me, can you hear me, Silas?"

Beulah got up from the steps and went to get him, and led him back. They sat down, and she put her arm around his shoulders, holding him like you do a little child.

"Where was the law?" he said, looking up at Mapes. He was crying now. "Where was the law? Law said he cut in on the tractor, and he was the one who started the fight. That's law for a nigger. That's law." He looked at Mapes. He wanted Mapes to face him. Mapes wouldn't. Mapes sucked on his candy. "How can a man on a wagon with mules—made of flesh and blood—cut in on a tractor, a machine? Ain't no way. No way. But that's what they said. And in my fear," Tucker said, looking at the rest of us, "in my fear, even after I had seen what happened—in my fear, I went along with the white folks. Out of fear of a little pain to my own body, I beat my own brother with a stalk of cane as much as the white folks did."

He looked at all of us, one after another. He wanted us to pass judgment over him for what he had done. Us judge him? How could any of us judge him? Who hadn't done the same thing, sometime or another?

We stayed quiet. Mapes was quiet. His little deputy was quiet. No air was stirring, so the trees, the bushes, everything was quiet.

Then Yank spoke. Mapes jerked his head around to look at Yank. He had thought the talking was over. He started to say something to Yank, maybe even wanted to cuss him. But he didn't, just looked at him, long and hard. Yank didn't pay him any mind.

"That's right," he said. "Anybody needed a horse broke, they called on Yank. In the parish, out the parish, they called on Yank. Anytime they needed a horse broke for a lady they called Yank, 'cause they knowed I knowed my stuff. Lot of these rich white folks you see riding these fine horses in Mardi Gras parades, prancing all over the place, I broke them horses. I, Sylvester J. Battley—me. Mathu, Rufe, Tucker, Gable, Glo there, they can 'count for that." He turned to Mathu. Mathu was nearly a foot taller than Yank; Mathu, tall and straight; Yank, short, stocky, and bowlegged. He looked up at Mathu, his brownish weak eyes pleading with Mathu to go along with what he was saying. Mathu nodded. Didn't say a thing, didn't even look down at him, just nodded. But that was good enough for Yank. "I broke all the horses, all the mules," he said. He wasn't talking to us now. He was thinking back, back when he was a younger man, when he used to do all this. "I broke 'em all. I broke Snook and Chip for Candy. Chip almost killed me when he throwed me 'gainst that fence. But I got back up. It had to be me or him. He's up in that pasture right now, too old to do nothing but eat grass. But you go up there and ask him who broke him—go on."

He stopped again. He nodded his head thoughtfully. He was still thinking back back.

"They ain't got no more horses to break no more. The tractors, the cane cutters—and I ain't been nothing ever since. They look at you today and they call you trifling, 'cause they see you sitting there all the time not doing nothing. They can't remember when you used to break all the horses and break all the mules. Snook, Chip, Diamond, Job. I broke Tiger, Tony, Sally, Dot, Lucky, Cora, John Strutter, Lottie, Hattie, Bird, Red, Bessie, Mut, Lena, Mr. Bascom. For Dr. Morgan, I broke Slipper, Skeeter, Roland. I broke 'em all. But the ones around here now don't remember that. Well, I remember. I remember. And I know who took it from me, too."

"You ever heard of progress?" Mapes asked him. Mapes had been wiping his face and neck again.

"I ain't thinking 'bout no progress. I'm thinking 'bout breaking horses," Yank said.

"You couldn't break a horse now if your life depended on it," Mapes said. He put the handkerchief back in his pocket. The handkerchief wasn't white anymore; it was gray now, and dirty.

"Maybe I can't break no more horses," Yank said. "Maybe that's why I shot the man who took the horse from me."

"Remember that for the record, Griffin," Mapes said, over his shoulder.

"I got it," Griffin said. "Yank. Y-a-n—"

"Sylvester J. Battley," Yank said. "Be sure and spell Sylvester and Battley right, if you can. When my folks read about me up North, I want them to be proud."

"How much more of this you going to take, Sheriff?" Griffin asked.

"Go on, tell him, Sheriff," Jacob said to Mapes. "I don't think that little fellow knows what's going on yet."

Mapes looked at Jacob a second; then he turned to Griffin. "Go check on Russell," he said. "See if he made it back there. Tell him to stay there. This might take a while."

That little spare-butt, slack-pants deputy left the yard, walking all tough like he was ready to take somebody in. He probably couldn't take Snookum to jail, if Snookum wanted to give him a fight.

After he was on the radio a few minutes, he came on back in the yard and told Mapes that Russell had made it back there and Russell said everything was all right for now. Mapes told him to go back, get on the radio, and tell Hilly to patrol the highway along Marshall and don't let anything suspicious come down here. That little deputy took in a deep breath and went back to the road talking to himself.

I had been watching that little deputy so much I didn't hear Gable when he first started speaking. He spoke so softly you had to be right on him to hear him. It was Glo I heard first. I heard her saying: "Careful, Gable. You know your heart. Careful, now."

Gable was standing on the other side of the steps, near Glo. He didn't stay at Marshall; he stayed at Morgan. Near Big Man Bayou, in a little shotgun house, behind the willows there at Morgan. He had been staying there by himself some fifteen, twenty years. He went to church twice a month—Determination Sunday and Sacrament Sunday. You hardly seen him any other time. Just staying there behind them trees there at Morgan. Had his little garden, a few chickens—staying behind them trees. Last person in the world any of us woulda expected to see today was Gable.

"He wasn't but sixteen years old, half out his mind, still

they put him in the 'lectric chair on the word of a poor white trash. They knowed what kind of gal she was. Knowed she had messed around with every man, black or white, on that river. But they put him in that chair 'cause she said he raped her. Even if he did, he was still no more than sixteen years old, and they knowed he was half out his mind."

"Be careful, Gable," Glo told him. She reached out her hand to touch his arm, but he was too far away from her.

"Called us and told us we could have him at 'leven, 'cause they was go'n kill him at ten. Told us we could have a undertaker waiting at the back door if we wanted him soon as it was over with. Is that something to say to a mother? Something to say to a father? 'Come get him at 'leven, 'cause we go'n kill him at ten'—that's something to say to—"

His voice choked, and he stopped. I wouldn't look at him. I was thinking back. It was '31 or '32—I believe '32. Huey Long was in Washington at that time.

I heard Glo again: "Be careful, Gable. Be careful, now."

"Saying how they hit that switch and hit that switch, but it didn't work. And how when they unstrapped him and took him back to his cell, how he thought he was already dead and in Heaven. Monk Jack was a colored trustee, and Monk Jack said the boy said: 'This here Heaven I'm in? Hanh? This Heaven? Y'all, this Heaven?' Said the boy said: 'Hi, Mr. So-and-So. Hi, Mr. So-and-So. Y'all made Heaven, too?' Said he said: 'Thank the Lord it's over with. And it didn't do no more than tickle me some. Didn't hurt at all.' Monk Jack said they told him: 'No, nigger, you ain't dead yet. But give us time.'

"Monk Jack told us how they throwed the boy back in the cell, and how they started hitting and kicking and cussing that 'lectric chair to make it work. Two of them doing this while another one come outside and told me and the undertaker we could go back of town if we wanted to, 'cause it was go'n take a while yet. Saying that to me, his paw, while two more was in there hitting and kicking and cussing that thing to make it work."

"Gable, your heart," Glo said, trying to reach him. But he was still too far away from her.

"Monk said you could hear one, then the other one, cussing that chair all over the courthouse. Not one of them round there knowed what to do, and they had to send get somebody from Baton Rouge to come fix it. Then they brought the boy out, strapped him in, and pulled the switch. Monk said after it was all over with, them white folks walked out of that room like they was leaving a card game. They wasn't even talking about it. It wasn't worth talking about.

"And what did I do about them killing my boy like that? What could a poor old nigger do but go up to the white folks and fall down on his knees? But, no, no pity coming there. Some went so far to say my boy shoulda been glad he died in the 'lectric chair 'stead at the end of a rope. They said at least he was treated like a white man. And it was best we just forgot all about it and him.

"But I never forgot, I never forgot. It's been over forty years now, but every day of my life, every night of my life, I go through that rainy day again.

"And that's why I kilt Beau, Mr. Sheriff," Gable said to Mapes. "He was just like that trashy white gal. He was just like them who throwed my boy in that 'lectric chair and pulled that switch. No, he wasn't born yet, but the same blood run in all their vein."

It was quiet after Gable got through talking. Even the children on the steps didn't move. You couldn't hear a bird, any kind of sound on the whole place. Mapes even kept the candy in his mouth still. The only thing that moved was the shadow from the house. It covered the yard now.

The deputy came back in the yard and told Mapes that Hilly was go'n keep a close lookout at the front. Mapes didn't look at him; he started moving the candy around in his mouth again. He was waiting for somebody else to say something.

"Can I speak?" Jameson asked Mapes.

Jameson was standing all by himself over by the far end of the garry. He wanted Mapes to know he wanted no part of us. Still Mapes looked at him like he hated him, too. Them ashes-color gray eyes looked hard as steel.

"I didn't know I was still in control here," he said.

"Ain't you the sheriff?" Jameson said.

"What's that got to do with it?" Mapes asked him.

"Get a gun if you want to talk, Jameson," Clatoo said, from where he was sitting on the garry.

"No, Mr. Clatoo," Jameson said. "I won't get a gun."

"Then you better shut up," Clatoo said. "People with guns speak first here today."

"So she made you the leader?" Mapes asked Clatoo.

Clatoo didn't even look at him. And there ain't nothing a white man hate more than for a nigger not to look at him when he speak to him.

Clatoo looked at Coot. "Coot, look like you was getting ready to say something?"

Coot was there in his old First World War Army uniform. The uniform was all wrinkled and full of holes, but Coot wore it like it was something brand new. He even had on the cap, and the medal. Any other time the people woulda been laughing at Coot dressed up like that.

"I shot him," Coot said.

"So did my grandmon," Mapes said.

"I was the only man from this parish ever fit with the 369th," Coot said. He didn't even look at Mapes. He was over by the garden fence, looking down the quarters toward the fields. "The 369th was a all-colored outfit. You couldn't fight side by side with these here white folks then. You had to get your training in France, take orders from French officers. They trained us good, and we helt our ground. Boy Houser, Minnycourt, Champagne—we helt our ground. We got decorated, kissed on the jaw—all that. And I was proud as I could be, till I got back home. The first white man I met, the very first one, one of them no-English-speaking things off that river, told me I better not ever wear that uniform or that medal again no matter how long I lived. He told me I was back home now, and they didn't cotton to no nigger wearing medals for killing white folks. That was back in World War One. And they ain't change yet—not a bit. Look what happened to Curt's boy when he come home from World War Two. Because they seen him with that German girl's picture, they caught him—and all y'all remember what they did to him with that knife. Korea—the same thing. That colored boy had throwed his body on that grenade to protect his platoon. Still the politicians here wouldn't let them bury him in Arlington like the rest of them was buried there. Vietnam, the same thing. It ain't changed. Not at all."

When Coot was talking to you, he had this habit of rocking back and forth. Sitting or standing, he rocked back and forth, back and forth. Sometimes he would stop talking awhile, but he would never stop his rocking.

"I used to put on my old uniform and look at myself in the chifforobe glass. I knowed I couldn't wear it outside, but I could wear it round the house. Today I told myself I was go'n put it on and I was go'n sit out on my garry with my old shotgun, and I was go'n shoot the first person who laughed at me or told me I had to take it off. I sat there and sat there; nobody passed the house. After a while I told myself I felt like having me a rabbit for supper tonight, and I started out for the swamps. But after I hit that Poland Road, looked like something just started pulling me this way. Didn't know what it was, but I couldn't make my old feets go no other way but toward Marshall."

Coot was looking at Mapes now, but Mapes would not look back at him. Mapes was looking across Mathu's garden, up the quarters. Maybe Coot had been telling the truth a second ago when he said he had put on his old uniform and went out on the garry, but Mapes knowed he was lying about the rest of it.

Coot went on: "I was sitting here on the garry when he jumped that ditch with that gun. I told him—I said, 'Hold it there, boy. Hold it there, now.' But did he listen? It wasn't nothing but a old nigger talking. Just another old nigger. Like them Germans thought. Them niggers won't dare shoot us—we white. The 369th left lot of them laying in them trenches with stupid grins on they faces."

Coot went on rocking another minute after he finished talking. He was proud of his little speech. He looked at us to see how we felt. I nodded to him. Couple other people nodded to him. He was proud the people had listened to him.

"Look down here, Jesus," Jameson said, looking at us. "Look down here, please."

"He's probably on their side," Mapes said.

"Don't talk like that," Jameson said to Mapes. "Don't blaspheme Him at a time like this. Look like you ought to be doing your duty."

"What do you want me to do?" Mapes asked Jameson. "Want me to take Mathu in? You think I want this whole bunch of Medicare patients in Bayonne? With that crowd out there already getting drunk for that big game tomorrow?"

"What you go'n do, just stay here and wait for Fix and his crowd?" Jameson asked Mapes.

"Maybe I'll have some luck," Mapes said.

"The only luck you might have is they don't kill everybody," Jameson said.

"Old bootlicker, shut up," Beulah said to Jameson.

Jameson was a good ten, fifteen feet away from Beulah. Now he started toward her. But he wasn't halfway before

Beulah had jumped up from the steps and was waiting for him. She had balled her fists, and now she was winding them over and over, waiting for him. Jameson stopped quicker than he had started.

"Come on, come on, you bootlicker," Beulah said. She was winding her fists over and over. "I'll whip you crazier than you already is, or I'll put some sense in your head—one. Come on. You think Mapes knocked you down—you just come on here. Old possum-looking fool."

"Take it easy, Reverend," Mapes said.

"Can I shoot him, Dirty Red?" Rooster asked. "Or should I just let my wife beat him?"

"Neither one of y'all do him anything," Dirty Red said. "Let Snookum beat him if he open his mouth again. You'll take care that little business for us, Snookum?"

Snookum glanced at his grandmother to see how she felt, but from the way Glo looked back at him, he knew he had better keep quiet.

Mapes went to Jameson and put his arm round his shoulders.

"Why don't you go home, Reverend?" he said.

"This is my place," Jameson said, still looking at Beulah. He said it so quiet you couldn't hardly hear him. He looked up at Mapes. "This is my place, Sheriff."

"Suit yourself," Mapes said, and dropped his arm from Jameson's shoulder.

"Anybody else got any more to say?" Clatoo asked.

Nobody answered. Mapes waited a second; then he started looking around.

"You mean y'all ran out of stories?" he asked. "And I thought you were just getting warmed up."

"Nobody ain't run out of nothing," Beulah said. She went on looking at Jameson a while before she turned to Mapes. "You want me to start?" she asked Mapes. "You want any woman here to start? I can tell you things done happened to women round here make the hair stand on your head. You want me to start? All you got to say is yes. All you got to do is nod."

"No," Mapes said. "I don't care to listen to any more of these tall tales." He looked around at all of us. "So this is payday, huh? And it's all on Fix, huh? Whether he had anything to do with it or not, Fix must pay for everything ever happened to you, huh?"

"He did his share of dirt," Beulah said.

"Fix didn't rise up in the Senate to keep that boy out of Arlington," Mapes said. "He never pulled the switch on that electric chair." He turned to Bing and Ding, the two mulattoes standing close together. "And you, Ding," he said. "That woman who poisoned your sister's child was Sicilian, not Cajun. She had nothing to do with Fix."

"She lived on that river," Ding said. "And he lived on that river. What's the difference?"

"That river, that river," Corrine said.

Everybody looked around. Nobody expected to hear anything from her. She hadn't said one word since she'd been there, just sitting in that rocker, gazing out in the yard. She hadn't moved but just one time since she had been there—to bring that spread to cover up Beau. Most of us had forgot she was even there.

"That river," she said again. "Where the people went all these years. Where they fished, where they washed they clothes, where they was baptized. St. Charles River. Done gived us food, done cleaned us clothes, done cleaned us soul. St. Charles River—no more, though. No more. They took it. Can't go there no more."

She stopped. Never raised her head. Still gazing out there in the yard.

"I can't do what I used to do on that river myself," Mapes

told her. But she wasn't listening. Maybe she didn't even know Mapes was there. "I can't fish on that river like I used to," Mapes said. "I can't hunt on that river like I used to. You blaming Fix for that, too? Then you blaming the wrong person. He's as much victim of these times as you are. That's why he's back on that bayou now, because they took that river from him, too."

Corrine went on gazing out in the yard. I don't think she even heard Mapes.

But Beulah heard him. "He was on that river at one time," she said. "And he sure did his share of dirt while he was there. Like drowning them two little children up the road."

"You're talking about thirty-five, forty, fifty years ago, Beulah," Mapes said. "And you got no proof Fix was mixed up in that."

"Now, ain't that just like white folks?" Beulah said to us, but still looking at Mapes. "Black people get lynched, get drowned, get shot, guts all hanging out—and here he come up with ain't no proof who did it. The proof was them two little children laying there in them two coffins. That's proof enough they was dead. Least to black folks it's proof enough they was dead. And let's don't be getting off into that thirty-five, forty, fifty years ago stuff, either. Things ain't changed that much round here. In them demonstrations, somebody was always coming up missing. So let's don't be putting it all on no thirty-five, forty, fifty years ago like everything is so nicey-nicey now. No, his seeds is still around. Even if he is old now, the rest of them had their hands in some of that dirt."

"Then you know more than I do," Mapes said.

"When it come to the kind of dirt been slung in this black woman's face—yes, sir, Sheriff, I reckon I do know more than you do."

"And you'll do anything to make me take you to jail, is that it?"

"If you take Mathu, you taking me," Beulah said.

"I'm taking Mathu, sooner or later," Mapes said. "And I'll make room for you."

"I'll be ready," Beulah said. "Just let me go home and put on my clean dress."

"I'll find a dress you can wear," Mapes said. "And I'll find a bucket and a mop, too."

"I ain't no stranger to buckets and mops," Beulah said. "Hoes, shovels, axes, cane knives, scythe blades, pickets, plows—and I can handle a gun, too, if I have to. I been in the pen before."

"You keep it up," Mapes said, "and you'll damned sure be going back." He turned to Glo sitting on the steps. "And you, Glo?" he said. "And them children?"

"I'm ready to go," Glo said. "I'll find somebody to look after them children."

"I don't know about Toddy, but I'm ready to go," Snookum said. He cracked his knuckles. "Wish I was just a little older so I coulda shot him."

"I thought you did," Mapes said. "Or was it you who went up to the front and called everybody?"

"I ain't got no more to say," Snookum said. "You can beat me with a hose pipe if you want."

He lowered his head. Mapes looked down at him awhile; then he nodded and turned to Candy. Candy was standing next to Mathu, who had sat down on the end of the step.

"That's how you organized it, all or none, huh?"

"I shot him," Candy said.

"You letting them all call you a liar right in front your face?"

"They're doing it to protect me," she said.

"Sure," Mapes said. "But before this day is over, don't be surprised, now, if you find your name on the same list with Fix's."

"You'd like that, wouldn't you?" Candy asked him.

"I can't think of anything I'd like better," Mapes said. He turned to his deputy. "Go check with Russell."

"Again?" the deputy said. "Why don't we just throw that old coon in the back of the car and take off?"

Everybody looked at that little deputy, but Candy looked at him harder.

"Go check with Russell like I said," Mapes told him.

That little deputy looked at Mapes, shook his head, and left the yard.

"You better warn that boy," Beulah told Mapes. "That's if you want him around much longer."

"He's sure got a big mouth for somebody with hardly any butt," Yank said, from over by the garden. "Pardon me, ladies."

"Forget it," Mapes said. "We're all one big happy family, aren't we?" he said to Candy.

Candy didn't answer him. She laid her hand on Mathu's shoulder, soft like touching a flower. Mathu's face never changed much, but he smiled when Candy touched him.

"Do you need to lie down?" she asked him.

He shook his head.

Candy looked at Mapes. "He hasn't been feeling too well lately. Suffering from those dizzy spells."

Mapes nodded. "Sure," he said. "I suffer from dizzy spells, too, every time I shoot somebody." He looked over his shoulder toward the road. "Well?" he called.

"All quiet," the deputy called back.

"The quiet before the storm," Mapes said to Lou. "He'll be here when he get them all together."

"We'll be here, too," Clatoo said, from the garry.

Thomas Vincent Sullivan

a k a

Sully or T.V.

Gil and I had just come out of Sci-210 when Cal caught up with us and told Gil that coach wanted him in the office right away.

"I thought we had gone over all that," Gil said.

"I don't think it's football this time," Cal said.

Gil asked me if I would walk back to the gym with him, and since Cal wasn't doing anything that hour he walked back with us. Cal was Calvin "Pepper" Harrison, quite possibly the best halfback in the country that year, and already nominated for All-American. Gil was Gilbert "Salt" Boutan, definitely the best fullback in the Southeastern Conference, and many other conferences besides. Cal and Gil were known as Salt and Pepper at LSU. Gil being a Cajun, the publicity people had tried to think of a good Cajun nickname for him when he first came to the university, but after seeing how well he and Cal worked together, they finally settled on Salt and Pepper.

Gil was a football man all the way, and eventually he would

go pro, but what he wanted most while attending LSU was to be All-American along with Cal. It would be the first time this had ever happened, black and white in the same backfield—and in the Deep South, besides. LSU was fully aware of this, the black and white communities in Baton Rouge were aware of this, and so was the rest of the country. Wherever you went, people spoke of Salt and Pepper of LSU. Both were good powerful runners, and excellent blockers. Gil blocked for Cal on sweeps around end, and Cal returned the favor when Gil went up the middle. It drove the defense crazy, because both Gil and Cal carried the ball about the same number of times in a game and the defensive team didn't know which to look out for. Besides that, you had "Sugar" Washington at quarterback, and he was no slouch, either.

Me? Well, I was no Sugar Washington. I was third-string quarterback. My name is Thomas Vincent Sullivan. My hair is red, my face is red, my eyes are green, and most people call me Sully. Others call me T.V.—especially the black guys on the team. Not for my initials necessarily, but for my avocation. I'm a television nut. A vidiot.

While Gil was in coach's office, Cal and I stood outside talking about the game coming up the next day, LSU and Ole Miss. It would be the game of the year. We knew if we dumped her, nobody else could stop us, and we would host the Sugar Bowl game on New Year's Day. Already the people had filled all the motels and hotels from Baton Rouge to New Orleans. The national press was covering the game. No matter where you went, that's all the people were talking about. If you were pro-LSU—and you were crazy if you were not—they said there was no possible way to stop Salt and Pepper. If you were anti-LSU, or pro-Ole Miss—and there were thousands of people from Mississippi who had come down for the game—they said that all Ole Miss had to do was stop one or the other, Salt or Pepper, and victory would be theirs to take back home. This kind of talk had been going on the past month, and now there was only a little more than twenty-four hours—thirty hours—before the whole thing would be settled. If you know anything about Louisiana weather, you know there's a lot of lightning and thundering before the big storm comes. Well, the big storm was going to be tomorrow night at eight o'clock, but the lightning and thundering had been going on for a month already, and nobody expected it to let up till the last moment.

After being in coach's office about ten minutes, Gil came back out, and went right by Cal and me like we weren't even standing there. I thought he had forgotten where he had left us, and I called to him. But he kept on going. Cal and I looked at each other a second, and went after him. He was walking fast, and rubbing both his fists.

"Gil, wait up," I said to him. "Hey, Gil."

Cal was on one side, I was on the other.

"What's the matter, man?" Cal asked him.

He had stopped. He was breathing sharp and hard, the way you do in the huddle after you've been tackled. He was staring down at the ground, rubbing his fists, rubbing his knuckles hard, like he was trying to rub off the skin.

Cal put his hand on one shoulder, and I took the other arm.

"What's the matter, Gil?" I asked him.

He started shaking his head; he was still looking down at the ground.

"My brother, my brother. Killed."

"In a wreck?" Cal asked him.

Gil went on shaking his head like he might start crying. I held on to one of his arms, and Cal was patting him on the back to console him. Then suddenly he just turned against Cal. Out of the blue, he looked at Cal like he suddenly hated him. It surprised the hell out of both me and Cal.

"Gil, that's Cal," I said. "Gil."

He turned from Cal and looked at me. "Why today?" he said. He was crying now. "Why today?"

"Take it easy, Gil," I said. People had begun to crowd around us and ask questions. Cal or Gil couldn't sneeze but there wasn't a crowd around. "Take it easy," I said to him.

"I have to get home," he said. "Can I borrow your car? Mine's still in the shop."

"I'll drive you," I said. "I can skip that drama class."

"Why today, Sully?" he asked me. "Why?"

I didn't know how to answer him, and I looked at Cal. Cal was just standing there looking hurt. He didn't know why Gil had turned against him, and I didn't know either.

"Let's go," Gil said.

"That's Cal, Gil," I said.

"Come on, let's go," he said, and walked away.

I followed him, but it sure made me feel bad the way he treated Cal.

I had a '68 Karmann-Ghia parked on the other side of the gym. Driving across campus, I had to drive about one mile an hour because of all the loonies who recognized Gil and wanted to wish him well in the game the next day. These were not all students, either. Many of them were graduates who had already arrived for the game that wasn't for another thirty hours. Someone has said that Norman, Oklahoma, is the nuttiest town in this country over football, but if any place can get crazier than this one, I would like to see it—or maybe I would not, because it sure could be dangerous.

Gil kept his head down. He would not look out at the loonies. I was driving one mile an hour. About a dozen other cars driving one mile an hour behind me. Out on the Highland road, I could speed up some, driving about five miles an hour. Loonies all over the place. Tomorrow this time it would be twice as bad, three times as bad, four times as bad. If Gil ever made All-American, handsome as he was, he would own this town and all the women in it.

Gil was quiet all the time. I didn't know whether I should say anything, so I kept quiet, too. I was still thinking about Cal. It made me feel bad the way Gil had treated him. On the gridiron they depended on each other the way one hand must depend on the other swinging a baseball bat. I had never known Gil to be anything but a gentleman.

We had crossed the Mississippi River, and were on the main highway that would take us to his folks' place in St. Raphael Parish. I had left all the loonies, at least the ones walking around loose, so I could drive sixty now. But all the time, Gil just sat over there quiet, rubbing his fists and gazing out at the road. I stayed quiet, too, not knowing what to say. I never know what to say to people who lose someone in the family. Besides, I was still thinking about Cal.

"God, I hope none of them had anything to do with it," Gil said. He wasn't looking at me; he was still looking out at the road. "I hope for God's sake none of them did it."

"Who are you talking about?"

"The black people there at Marshall. That's where he was killed. I hope for God's sake none of them did it."

So that's why he went against Cal like that. Whether he had anything to do with it or not, he was guilty because of his color. Jesus Christ. Jesus Christ, man. The two of you work on that field together as well as any two people I've ever seen in my life work together, and because of this—Jesus H. Christ. Come on, Gil, I thought to myself, you're made of better stuff than that.

"You don't know my folks, Sully. So little you know about me."

I know about you, I thought. I know a hell of a lot about you. I didn't know this side of you, but I know a hell of a lot about you, and about old Fix, too. I've heard how he and his boys used to ride in the old days. I just didn't know *you* were like that.

We could have stayed on this road to within a couple of

miles of his folks' place, but as we were coming up to the junction that said St. Charles River, he told me to take that turnoff. It was a good straight road for about four miles, with the sugarcane fields on either side. Much of the cane had been cut, and far across the field on the right side of the road was that dark line of trees which was the beginning of the swamps. Gil was looking across the fields toward the swamps. He looked in that direction until we made the turn that took us along the St. Charles River. The river was grayish blue, and very calm. On the other side of the river, probably three-quarters of a mile away, I could see how small the cars looked moving on the road.

After going about half a mile along the river, Gil nodded for me to pull off the highway. I didn't know before then that his reason for not heading directly to his folks' place was that he first wanted to go to Marshall.

Just as we turned into Marshall Quarters, I noticed a patrolman's car parked beside the road. The patrolman, in his gray-blue uniform, got out of the car and raised his hand for us to stop. He came over to my car. He recognized Gil immediately.

"Gil," he said.

"Hilly," Gil said.

Hilly looked at me. He wasn't much older than we were. He had red hair and freckles. He didn't wear a cap or a tie. The two top buttons of his shirt were unfastened, and you could see the reddish hair just below his neck. He looked back at Gil.

"Mapes told me to keep out trouble, but I guess you're okay."

"Mapes still down there?" Gil asked.

"Yes."

"Thanks," Gil said.

"Be pulling for you tomorrow night," Hilly said. But soon

as he said it, you could see that he felt he had spoken badly.

"Thanks," Gil said, and we drove off.

Marshall Quarters was a narrow little country road, all white with dust, and weeds on both sides. The one or two old clapboard houses seemed deserted, causing the place to look like a Western ghost town. All you needed was a couple of tumbleweeds to come bouncing down the road. Halfway into the quarters I could make out a tractor and several cars. As we came closer, I recognized Lou Dimes's baby-blue Porsche with the white streak on the side. Lou Dimes had been a starting forward on LSU's basketball team about ten years ago, and he still came to most of the games. Sometimes he covered the games for the paper in Baton Rouge.

Gil nodded for me to park in front of the tractor. We hadn't been there half a minute when I saw a skinny little guy coming out of the weeds with a pistol dangling from his right hand. He was looking suspiciously at us until he recognized Gil; then you could see him smiling. He came over to the car to look inside at us.

"Didn't know it was you," he said. "Sorry what happened, Gil."

He looked at me and nodded, and I nodded back. I thought he looked too pale to be a policeman.

"You wanta speak to Mapes?" he asked Gil.

Gil and I got out of the car. Gil stopped to look at the tractor a moment; then we followed the deputy back toward the house.

But Gil and I stopped again. There in the yard and on the porch were all these old men with shotguns. Besides, there was the sheriff with a pump gun. Lou Dimes was with his woman, Candy. Three or four black women sat either on the porch or on the steps. Some little dirty-looking children sat on the steps with the women. Every last one of them was looking back at us. It was like looking into the *Twilight Zone*.

Remember that old TV play *Twilight Zone?* You would be driving through this little out-of-the-way town, and suddenly you would come upon a scene that you knew shouldn't be there—it was something like that. Something like looking at a Brueghel painting. One of these real weird, weird Brueghels.

The sheriff lowered his pump gun when he recognized Gil. The rest of them did the same. You could see all those old shotguns being lowered an inch or two toward the ground.

Gil stepped across the little grassy ditch into the yard, and I was no more than a step behind him. The grass from his footsteps had not sprung back up before I was pressing it back down. And I intended to keep it that way until we got out of there.

"Gil." The sheriff spoke first. He was one of those great big guys, exactly what the people up North and in Hollywood thought a small-town Southern sheriff would look like.

Gil didn't answer him. I nodded to Dimes and Candy. Dimes spoke, but Candy didn't. She stood by the steps next to an old guy in a dirty tee shirt and green pants. She seemed lost in her own thoughts. She seemed no more interested in Gil and me than she did in anything else around her, except for that old guy, maybe. I had seen her at few of the games with Dimes, and she always seemed bored with everything. She acted like that now, bored. She also looked very tired.

"Where is my brother, Mapes?" I heard Gil asking.

"They took him into Bayonne," Mapes said.

Gil was looking at Mapes. He didn't think Mapes had told him enough. He wanted to hear more without asking for it. He didn't think, in a situation like this, it was necessary to ask.

"You're on your way home?" Mapes asked Gil. He was trying to show sympathy. But that was hard to do with a face and eyes like his.

Gil didn't answer this time either. He was doing everything

he could to control himself. He wanted the sheriff to say more about his brother.

"I got Russell back there on the bayou," Mapes said. "I told him to keep your daddy back there. I don't want him here at Marshall, Gil. I don't want him in Bayonne till I send for him."

The sheriff said all of this gently, with as much sympathy as anybody could who looked like he did. His face was big, red, with heavy jowls; his eyes were the color of cement. Even when he was trying to be gentle, his eyes still remained hard and staring at you.

Gil stared back at him. He was waiting for the sheriff to tell him more about what had happened.

"I'll have it over with before sundown," Mapes said. "You can take my word."

"What over with, Mapes?" Gil asked. He was doing all he could to control himself. "What over with, Mapes?"

"The person who did it—I'll have him in jail before sundown, I guarantee that," Mapes said.

"Don't you know who did it?" Gil asked.

"I think I do," Mapes said. "I'm sure I do."

"Then why don't you arrest him?"

"They all say the same thing. They all claim they did it."

"But you know who did it?"

"Yes," Mapes said. "I know who did it. But the others threatened to come to town if I take him in. She says the same thing. I don't want this crowd in Bayonne. Not the way people are working themselves up for that game tomorrow. If you just come from Baton Rouge, you know what I'm talking about."

"What do you plan to do, Mapes?"

"I'll handle it my way."

"Your way?" Gil asked. "My brother been dead how long, four hours?"

"About four hours."

Gil looked at him the way you look at somebody who should be telling you much, much more. But instead of saying more, Mapes turned away. Gil started looking at the old men around him. His eyes finally settled on the one in the dirty tee shirt and green trousers, the one nearest Candy. He did not say anything to the old man for a while. The old man was looking out over the road.

"You, Mathu?"

"Yes," the old man said, without looking at Gil.

Gil's right hand slowly tightened into a fist. Not that he wanted to hurt the old man. His face didn't show hatred or anger—just disbelief in the dry, direct way that the old man had answered him. If the old man had dropped his head and muttered out the words, that might have made a difference. But no, dry and direct, without even looking at Gil: "Yes, I did it."

"Ask the others," Mapes said. "Ask Candy."

Gil was still looking at old Mathu. The old man was not trying to avoid Gil's stare; he was just looking, thoughtfully, away from him.

Mapes held the pump gun in one hand, and he laid his big arm around Gil's shoulders.

"Go home, Gil," he said gently. It was said as gently as someone with a face and eyes like his could say it. Not necessarily as gently as it could be said in a situation like this.

Gil was still looking at old Mathu. He showed no sign that he had even heard Mapes.

"Gil," Mapes said, shaking him a little. "Gil."

Gil looked at him. "What is going on here, Mapes?" he asked. He said it as if he had just come into the yard and didn't know a thing. "What is going on here?"

"What is going on?" Mapes asked himself.

He looked around at the old men with the guns. Maybe he

knew the answers, maybe he didn't. But if he did, he didn't know how to explain it to Gil. Or maybe he didn't know how to put it so Gil could understand it. "Go home, Gil," he said.

Gil knocked Mapes's arm from his shoulders. Now he turned to Candy, who stood beside old Mathu. Up to now she hadn't shown any interest in our being there.

"What is going on here, Candy?" Gil asked her.

She raised her head slowly to look at him. She looked tired. But she showed no sympathy for him at all. She told him how Beau and somebody called Charlie had gotten into a fight back there in the fields. This Charlie fellow had run up to the front, and Beau had come after him with a gun. She was here talking to old Mathu. She told Beau not to come into the yard. She said she told him more than once not to come into the yard. He came in with the gun ready to shoot, and she stopped him. These other people heard about it and thought there would be trouble, and had come here to stand with her. She said she had already said all of that to Mapes.

"You're lying, Candy," Gil said. "Beau never would have come after Charlie with a gun. A stick, a stalk of cane, but never with a gun. Why are you saying all this? Why are you here in the first place? Why are all these old people here, Candy? To do what?"

She didn't answer him. She looked past him. She had made her point. She wasn't talking anymore.

Gil turned to Lou Dimes, who stood beside Candy.

"What's going on here, Lou?" Gil asked. "I know I can trust you. What's going on here?"

Lou was standing there beside Candy looking very uncomfortable. You could see he didn't like being here; he didn't like what was going on. He shook his head.

"I don't know, Gil," he said.

"Sure, you do," Gil said. I thought Gil was about to cry. "What's going on, Lou? Tell me what's going on."

"Gil, believe me," Lou said. "I don't know any more than what you see before you right now. Please believe me." He looked at me. "Why don't you take him home?"

"Come on, Gil," I said, and took him by the arm. But that was like pulling on a tree.

Gil turned back on Candy. "You never did like Beau," he said. "You never liked any of us. Looking at us as if we're a breed below you. But we're not, Candy. We're all made of the same bone, the same blood, the same skin. Your folks had a break, mine didn't, that's all."

She looked past him, like he wasn't even there. She looked tired, but other than that she showed no other expression.

"My God," Gil said. "My God, my God. Candy, if you only knew how sad, how pathetic you look."

She pretended not to even hear him. And maybe she didn't.

"Come on, Gil," I said, pulling on his arm again.

"Won't it ever stop?" he asked. He looked around at all of them. "Won't it ever stop? I do all I can to stop it. Every day of my life, I do all I can to stop it. Won't it ever stop?"

The people did not look at him. They were not looking down; they were just looking away.

"Come on," I told him. "Come on. Let's get out of here."

He looked around at all of them; then he turned quickly and walked away. And I followed him out of the yard.

Lou Dimes

I had noticed for the past hour that the people were leaving the front yard one at a time to go to the back. The only time they didn't move around was when Gil and that other fellow were here, but as soon as they left, the people started moving one at a time toward the back again. Each one would stay four or five minutes, return and nod, then another one would go. Mapes didn't pay them any attention, and neither did Candy.

Candy leaned back against the porch near the steps where Mathu was sitting, and I leaned back against the porch beside her. I asked her to go with me for a walk so we could talk. She said no. I asked her wouldn't it be better if she were at home. She said she would not leave. I told her that I would keep her posted on anything that went on around here. She said she was not leaving. I asked her why did she need me then. She said she just needed me. Mapes was on the other side of the steps. He showed no interest in what we were talking about. Just like all the rest of them around there, he seemed to be waiting for something. But what were they waiting for? For Fix to show up, or not show up? I didn't know what was going on. I was just there.

I went around the house to the back. I met one of the old fellows coming from the toilet. He had his gun as all the others did, but still he moved off the little path for me. We nodded to each other as we passed by.

The old fellow had been careful. They had all been careful. There were no water marks on the seat. Only some corncobs, the two backs of an old catalogue, some newspaper, a couple of paper bags. I didn't have any use for any of this, and after spitting into the hole, I went back out into the fresh air. Halfway up the path, I met Candy.

"Any spiders in there?" she asked me.

"I didn't see any. Some cobwebs. Why don't you go on home, Candy," I told her.

"Thanks," she said, and went by me.

"You want me to wait for you?" I asked her.

"No," she said. "Go on back to the front before he does anything stupid."

"Candy, you can't do anything good here," I said. "Why don't you go on home?"

She didn't answer. She had already gone inside the toilet. I went back to the front, and a few minutes later she returned and took her post next to Mathu. The people had left that same little space open for her. She and Mathu looked at each other, and she asked him how he felt. He told her he was all right. I caught Mapes looking at them, but he didn't say anything.

Then we saw the dust, but even before Mapes could nod to Griffin, Griffin was already leaving the yard with the pistol dangling in his hand. Mapes watched him carrying the pistol against his leg, and you could see that Mapes was going to get rid of Griffin first chance he got.

Everyone watched the dust rising over the weeds, but no one moved from his place. I supposed they figured that it was still too much light for Fix to show up, and even if he did, they would have time to scatter before he took aim. Mapes did not move either, just leaning kind of leisurely back against the end of the porch. He still had his gun, of course, and I did notice that his thumb was near the safety catch.

Griffin was in the ditch behind a clump of weeds, the pistol in the right hand, while the left hand separated several stalks of bloodweeds so that he could get a better look up the quarters. Then after a while he looked back at Mapes and nodded his head to let Mapes know that it was all right. Mapes's thumb touched at the safety catch of the gun, but from the way he was looking at Griffin, you knew he was going to get rid of Griffin as soon as all of this was over with, if not before.

I saw now why Griffin had nodded his head; it was Miss Merle. After stopping just a little past where the gate used to be, she sat in the car awhile watching us. She did it just the way everyone else had done it, even though this was her second time seeing it. Then she got out with a basket covered with a dish towel, and she was already fussing. The first person she came up to was Griffin, and she told him something, and Griffin went back to the car and got another basket covered with a dish towel, and came into the yard with the basket in one hand and the gun in the other, and you could see Mapes looking at him as if he were wondering if he actually needed Griffin the rest of the day. Miss Merle didn't come up to Mapes, or Candy, or me first, she started dishing out sandwiches to the first one she came to. I supposed she felt that since we were all conspirators together, one was no better than the others, so she just started dishing out the sandwiches to the first person she got to, and fussing all the time.

"Just look at this, I mean just look at this—just look at it." Dishing out sandwiches and fussing. "I hope you like ham and cheese, because there isn't anything else. Just look at that. I mean just look at that. Hurry up with that other basket," she said, over her shoulder to Griffin. Griffin brought her the full basket, and she handed him the empty one. So Griffin was standing there with an empty basket in one hand and a loaded revolver in the other. "Can't you put that thing away for a second?" Miss Merle asked him. "Who are you going to shoot, the hog?"

"No, Ma'am," Griffin said.

"Just look at that," Miss Merle said, looking at Griffin. Then she looked at the rest of us. "Just look at that."

She was dishing out sandwiches again. The sandwiches were neatly wrapped in wax paper. There were lettuce and tomatoes on the ham and cheese.

"And you," she said to Candy. "Just look at you. Just look at you."

Candy took the sandwich without looking Miss Merle in the face. Miss Merle shook her head disgustedly, and turned to Mapes.

"Here. You better have two. But there ain't no beer."

Mapes spat out a piece of white candy that was about as thick as a contact lens.

"Water is good," he said. "You don't mind, do you, Mathu?"

"Snookum, go get me that jug of ice water out the icebox," Mathu said. "And bring couple them jelly glasses out the safe."

Snookum left the porch eating. All the rest of us were eating. Not one there was not eating. Mapes, Candy, Mathu, Griffin, the old men, the old women, the children—everybody was eating. We were all hungry.

"You ever seen anything like it?" Miss Merle asked herself. "Have you? Lord, have mercy. Well?" she said to Mapes.

"They're good," Mapes said. "Who made them?"

"Janey and—" But she stopped. Now she just looked at him. Southern women, black or white, can look at you like that. Like they're thinking that you or they, one of you, should not be standing on the same planet at the same time.

"Do you see that sun?" she asked Mapes.

The house shadow had crossed the road where the tractor and trailers were.

"About another hour," Mapes said.

Snookum came back with the jug and glasses, and poured Mapes some water. Then he stood before Miss Merle, but she was paying too much attention to Mapes to notice him. She could not see how Mapes could stand there drinking water while all this was going on. She could not see how she and Mapes ended up being on the same planet at the same time.

"Have another one?" Snookum said to her.

She jerked around. "What?" she said angrily.

"Sammich," he said. "Candy didn't pay me nothing for going—" He glanced at Mapes and stopped.

Miss Merle did not try to figure out what he was talking about. She just looked at him like they did not belong on the same planet at the same time. Snookum held out his hand, waiting. His little black face dusty, his twisted little curls dusty, the little hand grimy. Miss Merle looked him up and down. She didn't want to feel pity. There were too many others deserving pity. Where would she stop?

"Here," she said, pushing a sandwich into his hand. "Now, get away from me."

"Lou can stand another one, too," Mapes said.

"What?" Miss Merle said, turning on Mapes.

Mapes went on chewing. The left corner of Miss Merle's mouth quivered from tension. She was sure God had made a mistake putting her here at the same time He did Mapes. Mapes was not thinking about it. He went on eating.

"Here," Miss Merle said to me. "Pass them out."

I put one of the sandwiches on the porch next to where I was standing; then I went around with the basket. Most of the people refused to take a second one. They were still hungry, but there were not enough sandwiches for everyone to have two, so most of the people declined a second one until the basket had made the round. Then Miss Merle took it from me and went to the different people who looked hungriest to her. She was still fussing.

"Just look at this. Jesus, will you just look at this. Here. Here. Lord, just look at this. Here, Clabber, Here, Clatoo. Dirty Red, take this. Jesus, will you just look at this."

She came back to the steps where Mapes was leaning leisurely back against the porch. His pump gun was propped against the steps.

"There is no dessert," she said. "There's not enough of that pie for all of you and—" She stopped. Why did she have to explain anything to anybody? Why did she even waste her time bringing us sandwiches? "Jesus, you ever seen anything like this in all your born days?" she asked herself. "You satisfied now, you and your army?" she suddenly turned on Candy.

Candy ate her sandwich while gazing down at the ground. She did not answer.

"How long is this charade going on?" Miss Merle snapped back at Mapes.

"They all claim they did it," Mapes said. "Who should I take in? Her?"

Miss Merle's little birdlike red mouth tightened and untightened two or three times. From her eyes, you could see that she was questioning God's reason for putting her here at the same time He did the rest of us. God did not answer her, so she turned on me.

"And you're supposed to be a man? What kind of husband will you make if you let her kick—" She stopped again. I would not look at her, but I could feel her staring at me. She probably wanted to hit me, she wanted to hit somebody, but she was too much of a lady. She turned on Mathu.

"Tell her to get her butt up the quarters," she said.

"Up to her," he said, chewing.

"Since when?" Miss Merle asked him.

Mathu never stopped chewing. He never looked at her either. But she continued looking at him. Not the way a white woman is supposed to look at a black man when giving him orders or advice. She looked at him the way any woman would look at any man when they have shared more than a few moments together.

Those shared moments were over the upbringing and training of Candy. After Candy's mother and father died in the car wreck, Miss Merle and Mathu realized that the other two at the house, her aunt and uncle, were not capable of bringing her up properly, and so took it as their duty to raise her themselves. One to raise her as a lady, the other to make her understand the people who lived on her place. And she had been as close to those two, Miss Merle and Mathu, as she had been to anyone in her life.

When Mathu refused to look back at Miss Merle, her little birdlike mouth tightened and untightened two or three times. Then she jerked around and looked at the rest of us.

"Let me get away from here," she said. "Where is my other basket?" She found Griffin, and jerked the basket out of his hand. "You all can do what you want," she said. "But don't come up to that house bleeding, because I'm not patching up anybody. Janey can't do it because she's hysterical. Bea can't because she's stone drunk."

"I'll walk with you out to the car," Mapes said.

"What for?" Miss Merle snapped at him. She drew back one of the baskets.

"Hold it," Mapes said, raising two fingers in the peace sign. "Just want to say thanks for the sandwiches."

Miss Merle stood there with the basket half cocked. Mapes would not dare grunt or grin. No one else did, either. I had the feeling that if she had made one sweep of that basket, everybody was going to scatter.

She shook her head. "No, I'm not going to hit anybody. I'm going home. If I stay down here any longer, I know I'll go mad."

She left the yard. Mapes caught up with her just as she

crossed the ditch. They stood by the car talking. After a while she got into the car and went farther down the quarters to turn around. When she had passed by the house again, I went out into the road where Mapes was. He was leaning back against his own car, looking at the people in the yard. I leaned back against the car next to him. It had gotten a little cool now that the shadows had covered everything. Mapes offered me a Life Saver. I shook my head. I knew there were only one or two left, and he would probably need them later.

"What's going to happen, Mapes?" I asked him.

"I don't know," he said. "I'm waiting for Russell to call me."

"Call you about what?"

"I don't know," he said.

"You don't seem to be in any great hurry."

"Nope," he said. He looked at Mathu sitting on the steps; then he looked up in the sky where the sun was an hour or so ago. "Too late to go fishing now anyhow," he said.

Sully

———

From Marshall to the Bayou Michel is about ten miles, five miles along the St. Charles River, and then you turn off the highway onto a blacktop road for another five miles. The Bayou Michel is then on your right, and houses on the left are facing the bayou. The road and bayou twist and turn like a snake. There's never more than a couple hundred yards of straight road before you have to go around another curve.

This was Cajun country. You had a few other whites, a few blacks, but mostly Cajuns, with names like Jarreau, Bonaventura, Mouton, Montemare, Boutan, Broussard, Guerin, Hebert, Boudreaux, Landreaux—all Cajun names. There were people back here with names like Smith and Kelly, and they claimed to be Cajuns, too, their fathers' having married Cajun women. The blacks on the bayou also spoke the Cajun French as well as English.

This was Gil's country. I had come back here with him a half-dozen times before, and it had always been pleasant. We would go hunting or fishing or just visit some of the people. Gil loved all the people back here, and they all loved him, white and black. He would shake a black man's hand as soon as he would a white man's, and the blacks would beam with pride when he did. But today I had not seen one black man, woman, or child since we left Marshall.

Gil, with his arm in the window, was looking out at the trees along the Bayou Michel. Most of the trees were weeping willows; their long, limp branches brushed against the ground and the surface of the water. Every now and then you would see a cypress, a sycamore, or some other kind of tree, but mostly willows, and lots of bushes. When there was a little space between the trees and bushes, you would see the dirty brown shallow water. No form of life was on the water itself. No animals, no birds, nothing green. Only twigs and dry leaves that had fallen from the trees along the bank. Gil was looking out of the window at the bayou, but never saying anything. He had not said a single word to me since we left Marshall.

We were coming up to his folks' place now, a great big white frame house with a screened-in porch, and screen over the doors and windows. There were quite a few cars and trucks parked in front of the place, so we had to go maybe a hundred yards before we could find room to park; then we got out and walked back. I saw a tall, sandy-haired fellow standing by a car watching us. He smiled as we came back.

"Gilly," he said.

"Russ," Gil said. Gil nodded toward me. "This is Sully."

Russ nodded. I nodded back. We shook hands.

Gil started looking around at all the trucks and cars parked before the house. A half-dozen men stood around one of the trucks in the yard.

"Waiting for you inside," Russ said to Gil.

"You coming in?" Gil asked him.

"I have to keep your daddy back here, Gil," Russ said.

"I'd like for you to come in, if you don't mind," Gil said.

"Sure, if you want me to," Russ said.

He reached into the car to get a necktie hanging over the stem of the rearview mirror. After he had made a good knot and drawn it tight, he stuffed his white shirt neatly into his gray pants, and reached back into the car to get his coat off the seat. The coat had been covering a revolver, a wooden-handled .38 special. He looked at the revolver a moment; then he put it inside the dash drawer and slammed the door shut. He passed his fingers through his long sandy hair, and we went into the yard.

The men in the yard spoke to Gil, but in a quiet, subdued way. You could see how much he was the hero among them, but there was no enthusiasm today. Gil nodded to most of them, and shook hands with a couple of them, but he did not stop to talk. The men didn't say anything to me or Russ. I stuck close behind Gil, and Russ was a step or two behind me. As we came up on the porch, I could hear people talking inside the house. Gil pulled the screen door and pushed open the wooden door, and we came into a room where there were at least three dozen people. Men, women, small children, all speaking either Cajun French or English.

"Bonjoure, Gi-bear," a little girl said to Gil.

Gil leaned over and kissed her. He shook hands with a couple more people; then he asked about his father. A big man wearing khakis nodded toward a door to the right. Russ and I followed Gil through the door and into another room. This room was not as crowded—maybe a dozen people. All men except two women and a little boy. The two women sat on a four-poster brass bed which had a mosquito net at the head of it. One of the women had her head down and was crying, and the other one had her arm around her. Fix Boutan was sitting in a soft chair by the window, and the little boy was in his lap. Fix was a short man with a big head, broad shoulders, thick chest, and big hands. He had practically no neck at all, and his big head set on his shoulders the way a volleyball sits on a bench. He must have just come from the barbershop, because his gray hair was cut close on the sides, brushed straight back on top, and I could smell as well as see the oil in his hair. He probably had gone to the barber to get himself all prettied up for the big game the next day. He squinted up at Gil when we came into the room, and you could see that he had been crying.

"You got here," he said.

"Yes, Papa," Gil said, and kissed him on the side of the face.

Gil passed his hand over the head of the little boy who sat in Fix's lap; then he turned to the women on the bed. One could have been in her late teens, the other one was in her mid- or late twenties—she was the one crying. Gil leaned over and kissed her. He said something to her that I didn't understand; then after speaking to the younger woman, he spoke and shook hands with two or three of the other men in the room. The men shook hands, nodded, and spoke quietly. Gil turned back to Fix.

"Papa, I know this is a family matter, but Sully drove me down from Baton Rouge, and I asked Russ to come in, too."

Fix nodded to me. It was not the most enthusiastic nod I had ever received, but I could understand after what had happened today. He looked at Russ, but he didn't speak or nod to him. He looked back at Gil.

"Why you so late getting here?"

"I went by Marshall, Papa."

"You see him?"

"They had already taken him to Bayonne."

The woman on the bed who was crying lowered her head more. The other woman held her close. Fix looked at the two women, and looked back at Gil. The little boy in Fix's lap, who was four or five, laid his head against Fix's chest.

Gil sat on the bed beside the woman and clasped his hands

and looked down at the floor. Fix and the other men watched him.

"Well?" Fix said when Gil had not said anything for a while.

"He doesn't want you there, Papa," Gil said, looking up at Fix.

Fix squinted back at Gil. Several of the other men mumbled among themselves. Fix raised a big hand, not very high, and the men respected it.

"Don't want me where?" Fix asked Gil.

"Marshall, or Bayonne. Until he sends for you," Gil said.

"Mapes is crazy," one of them said.

"He's got to be crazy," someone else said.

"My boy laying dead in the morgue, shot down like a dog, and Mapes don't want me in Bayonne?" Fix asked Gil.

"He's crazy," one of the men said.

Fix looked at the man to shut him up. Fix had small dark pig eyes, and he didn't have to look at you very long or very hard to shut you up. He looked back at Gil.

"Mapes still at Marshall?"

"Yes, Papa," Gil said.

"What's he doing at Marshall?" Fix asked.

"Talking to the people," Gil said.

"Talking to the people about what? He don't know who did it?"

"He thinks Mathu did it."

"But why should Mathu kill my boy?"

"He claimed Beau came into his yard with a gun."

"What for?" Fix asked.

"He came after Charlie. He came with a gun."

"And Mathu killed him for that?" Fix asked.

"That's what Mapes believes."

"Ain't we wasting time, Fix?" a big, rough-looking guy standing in the back of the room asked Fix. He wore one of those Hawaiian shirts with all the red and blue and yellow flowers on it. The tail of the shirt was out of his pants. He stood next to another rough-looking guy, who wore a brown, short-sleeve shirt. Both wore khaki pants.

"Luke Will," Fix said. "You might have been a friend of Beau's. But you not a member of this family, and you don't speak."

"I was closer than a friend," Luke Will said. "I was a good friend. We had a beer last night."

"You still don't speak," Fix told him. "I speak. My sons speak. I tell you when to speak. That's clear, Luke Will?"

"I still say we're wasting valuable time," Luke Will said.

"You better go out, Luke Will, if you can't control your mouth," Fix told him.

Luke Will didn't move. Fix looked at him awhile; then he looked at the other big, rough-looking guy in the brown shirt, warning him, too. Fix turned back to Gil sitting on the bed.

"Well?" Fix said to him.

"Can I say something, Papa?" Gil said.

"I'm waiting," Fix said.

"Papa," Gil said, and leaned a little forward on the bed to look at him. "Papa," he said again. But he didn't say any more.

Fix looked at Gil, and patted the little boy on the leg. The little boy wore short blue pants and a white tee shirt. He didn't have on any shoes.

"Well?" Fix said to Gil.

"Papa," Gil said. "I went to Marshall."

"You said that," Fix said.

"I saw something over there, Papa—something you, I, none of us in this room has ever seen before. A bunch of old black men with shotguns, Papa. Old men, your age, Parrain's age, Monsieur Auguste's age, all with shotguns, Papa. Waiting for you."

"Niggers with shotguns waiting for me?" Fix asked. His dark piglike eyes opened just a little bit wider. He squeezed the little boy closer to his chest.

"Fifteen, and maybe even more," Gil said. "And Mapes there with a pump gun—all waiting for you."

"Then let's accommodate Mapes and his niggers," someone else said.

"Papa," Gil said, without ever looking around at the other person. "Old men, Papa. Cataracts. Hardly any teeth. Arthritic. Old men. Old black men, Papa. Who have been hurt. Who wait—not for you, Papa—what you're supposed to represent. Ask Sully. Tired old men trying hard to hold up their heads."

"What are you trying to say, Gi-bear?" Fix asked him.

Gil looked up at me to help him out. "Sully, please tell him," he said.

"I'm not talking to your friend there, Gi-bear, I'm talking to you," Fix said.

"Papa," Gil said. He rubbed the knuckles of both fists, trying to figure out a way to say it. When it came to running that ball, he ran it as well as anybody I'd ever seen in my life, but trying to tell his father what he felt inside of him was the hardest thing for him to do. "Papa," he said, leaning toward Fix with his hands clasped together. Fix waited. "Papa," Gil said. "All my life I have heard what my family have done to others. I hear it today—from the blacks, from the whites. I hear it from the opponents even when we play in another town. Don't tackle me too hard, because they would have to answer to the rest of the Boutans. It hurts me to hear that, Papa. It hurts me in here," he said, hitting his chest. "It hurts me because I know it's not true."

"What are you trying to say, Gi-bear?" Fix said. "Get to the point."

"Papa," Gil said, rubbing his knuckles again. "Papa, I want to be an All-American at LSU. I have a good chance—Cal and me. The first time ever, black and white, in the Deep South. I can't make it without Cal, Papa. I depend on him. Every time I take that ball, I depend on his block, or his faking somebody out of my way. I depend on him, Papa, every moment I'm on that field."

Fix watched him. Gil looked down at the floor, biting his bottom lip. Fix waited. The rest of the people waited. If anybody was breathing, they were doing it quietly. The little boy in Fix's lap laid his head against Fix's chest and sucked his thumb. Everybody waited for Gil to go on. The woman on the bed who had been crying was quiet. The younger woman kept her arm around her. The people in the other room were not talking as much as before.

Gil looked up at Fix.

"I couldn't make All-American, Papa, if I was involved in something against the law," he said. "Even if our name was involved, the Yankee press would destroy me." Gil leaned closer toward his father. "Papa, I'm not putting things right. I'm not saying what I want to say. But do you understand what I'm trying to say? Do you understand, Papa?"

"What about your brother, Gi-bear?" Fix asked. Those little dark pig eyes looked deadly at Gil. "What about Beau?"

"I loved my brother, Papa. He was much older than me, but we were very close. He taught me everything I know about fishing and hunting. I loved my brother, Papa. But Beau is dead. Nothing we can do will bring him back. You understand what I'm trying to say, Papa?"

Fix's little dark pig eyes still looked deadly at Gil.

"You through, Gi-bear?" he asked him.

"Papa, I won't go along," Gil said, shaking his head. "You can beat me, but I won't go along."

"I ask if you through, Gi-bear? You through?"

Gil took in a deep breath and nodded his head. And he looked down at the floor.

"What do you think of our great All-American there, Alfonze?" Fix asked. "Hanh, A-goose?"

He was speaking to the two old men sitting over to his right, but he was still looking at Gil. Neither one of the old men answered him. One shrugged his shoulders, but the other one didn't even do that much.

"And you, Claude?" Fix looked up at the man standing near the foot of the bed.

Claude was Gil's older brother. He drove a truck for an oil company in Lafayette. He was a big guy, six two, six three, with jet-black curly hair. He wore khakis, and you could see the sweat marks in the back of the shirt and around the armpit. He was cleaning his fingernails with a small pearl-handled knife. Even after Fix had spoken to him, he went on cleaning his fingernails.

"Whatever you say, Papa," he answered, without looking at Fix.

Fix nodded his head. "Jean?"

Jean was another of Gil's brothers. He didn't look anything like Gil or Claude—or Fix either, for that matter. He was short like Fix, but too pale. He was probably in his mid-thirties. He wore a black-striped seersucker suit, a white shirt, and a little bow tie. He glanced around nervously at the people nearest him; then he moved closer to Fix's chair. Fix was looking up at him, and patting the little boy on the leg.

"Papa, we ought to talk," Jean said.

"Then talk."

"What will we do when we go to Bayonne, Papa? Who will go to Bayonne?"

"You don't want to go to Bayonne?" Fix asked him.

"I live in Bayonne, Papa," Jean said. "My butcher shop is in

Bayonne. But who else is going to Bayonne?" He looked around at the men in the room, then back to Fix again. "And for what reason, Papa?"

"I go to see my boy," Fix said. "And your brother."

"And the rest of these, Papa," Jean said, nodding toward the men in the back of the room. "Why are they going to Bayonne?"

"Your brother was brutally murdered today," Fix said. "You forget so easily, Jean?"

"No, Papa, I don't forget so easily," Jean said. "I won't ever forget this day, ever. But Gilly is right. We have law out there to do what many of these people would like to see us do. Some of these in the room with us right now."

"These people are your friends. My friends, Beau's friends."

"If they're friends of the family, show respect to the family. Stay out of Bayonne until Mapes has cleared this up."

"Mapes will never clear this up," Luke Will said, from the back of the room. "Beau's been dead for hours, shot down like a dirty dog, and Mapes hasn't done a thing about it."

"Don't y'all listen to Luke Will," Russ said. Russ had been standing next to me, and he had been quiet all the time. "Don't listen to him. All he and that gang want is trouble."

"What gang's that, Russell?" Luke Will asked.

"You know what gang," Russ said, still looking at Fix.

"Scared to call their names?" Luke Will asked him. He grinned, a real mean grin, the kind of grin that comes from just the corner of the mouth.

"Everybody in here know who I'm talking about," Russ said. He never looked at Luke Will. "Don't listen to Luke Will, Fix. He's no friend."

"He's a friend," Fix said.

"Give the word, Fix," Luke Will said.

"What word is that, Luke Will?" Fix asked, looking back at him.

"We go to Marshall."

"That's my decision to make, Luke Will—and my sons'. Not yours."

Luke Will nodded. "All right, Fix. I'll wait your decision. Then I'll go to Marshall."

"Don't try it," Russ said, looking back at him for the first time.

Luke Will grinned at Russ. He was one of those big, hulking, beer-belly red-necks. He had long brown hair, and when he grinned from the side of his mouth, I could see that some of his teeth were missing. The guy standing next to him didn't look any better than Luke Will did, but at least he kept his mouth shut.

"I won't have none of that in my house," Fix said. "And you, Russell, I would be quiet if I were you."

"I'll do anything to keep you back here, Fix," Russ said. "And that goes for the rest of you," he said, looking around the room. He looked back at Fix. "I mean it, Fix," he said. "I have my orders."

"Russell," Fix said, pointing his finger at him. "You can't keep me back here. Only my sons can keep me back here. You remember that."

"Jean and Gilly are right," Russ said. "Luke Will is wrong. Luke Will wants trouble."

"In my house, I say what is right and what is wrong," Fix said, raising his voice now. He held the little boy with the left hand while he pointed the right hand at Russ. "I decide. Me, William Fix Boutan, I decide."

He stared at Russ to see if Russ had any more to say. Russ looked down at him, but remained quiet.

Fix turned to the old men sitting to his right. Both sat in their chairs erect as boards, listening, but staying quiet. The one nearest Fix wore a clean, ironed white shirt and khaki pants. His hat was on his knee. The other one wore a Hawaiian shirt with about six different colors in it. He wore white pants, and his hat hung on the back of his chair.

"What should I do, Alfonze?" Fix asked the one nearest him. His voice was calm again.

"I go along whatever you decide, Fix," the old man said.

"A-goose?" Fix asked the other one.

"I'm an old man, Fix," Auguste said. "I don't know who is right and who is wrong anymore."

"I'm an old man, too," Fix said. "Twenty years ago I would not have asked questions. I would have been at Marshall by now."

"I would have been at Marshall with you twenty years ago, Fix."

"They're old as we are," Fix said. "They're waiting for me—according to this All-American here."

"Old men with guns waiting for old men with guns, Fix, but isn't that a farce?" Auguste said.

"And Beau on that cold slab in Bayoone, A-goose? Is that a farce also?"

"I christened him," Auguste said. "I'm his parrain. You must know how I feel."

"Ain't we wasting time, Fix?" Luke Will asked, from the back of the room again.

"Jean and Gi-bear say no, Luke Will. Even my good friend A-goose says no."

"A-goose is an old man, and don't have all his senses," Luke Will said. 'Gilly and Jean want to keep their good names with the niggers. Gilly want to play football with niggers, mess around with them little stinky nigger gals. Beat Ole Miss tomorrow, that's what he wants. As for Mr. Jean there, he has to sell his hog guts and cracklings to the niggers. No decent white man would buy 'em."

"Is that so, Gi-bear?" Fix asked Gil. "Your brother's honor for the sake to play football side by side with the niggers—is that so?"

"Luke Will's days are over with, Papa," Gil said. "Luke Will's days are passed. Gone forever."

"And mine?" Fix asked him. "Mine, Gi-bear?"

"Those days are gone, Papa," Gil said, "Those days when you just take the law in your own hands—those days are gone. These are the '70s, soon to be the '80s. Not the '20s, the '30s, or the '40s. People died—people we knew—died to change those things. Those days are gone forever, I hope."

"What day is gone, Gi-bear?" Fix asked him. "The day when family responsibility is put aside for a football game? Is that the day you speak of, Gi-bear?"

"I'm not speaking of family responsibility, Papa," Gil said. "I'm speaking of the day of the vigilante. I'm speaking of Luke Will's idea of justice."

"So I'm a vigilante now, huh, Gi-bear?" Fix asked him.

"That's what Luke Will wants us to do," Gil said. "He and his gang still think the world needs them. The world has changed, Papa. Luke Will and his gang are a dying breed. They need a cause like this to pump blood back into their dying bodies."

"And Beau?" Luke Will asked Gil. He had to speak to Gil's back, because Gil would not give him the respect of looking round at him. "Beau," Luke Will said again. "He's more alive than I am at this moment?"

"Well, Gi-bear?" Fix asked.

"Beau is dead, and I'm sorry, Papa," Gil said. "But I would like people to know we're not what they think we are. They all expect us to ride tonight. They're all waiting for that. I say let them wait. Let them wait and wait and wait."

"And you there, Mr. Butcher of hog-gut fame?" Fix said, looking up at Jean.

"They want something to happen," Jean said, wiping his face with a handkerchief. He wiped the palms of his hands and put the handkerchief back. "I go along with Gilly."

Fix looked up at him, nodding his head; then he looked around at the rest of the people in the room.

"And the rest of you, how you feel?" he asked. "You feel that this, this butcher and this, this All-American got a point?"

"We're wasting time," Luke Will said.

No one else spoke out. They only mumbled among themselves. Neither Russ, Claude, nor I said anything. I was not about to open my mouth.

"Well, Gi-bear?" Fix asked.

"They'll listen to you, Papa," Gil said. "Make them see that it'll hurt the family. It'll hurt our name."

"But especially yours, huh, Mr. All-American?"

"It would hurt me, Papa. Yes."

Fix looked from Gil to the woman sitting on the bed with her head bowed. She had been quiet a long time, but never once raised her head to look at anyone. Fix looked at the little boy in his lap and patted him on the leg.

"You know this little boy I'm holding here?" he asked, looking back at Gil. "Tee Beau. No more papa." He looked at Gil awhile to let those words make an impression; then he nodded toward the woman on the bed. "You know that lady sitting there—Doucette? Huh? No more husband."

"I'm sorry, Papa," Gil said. "I'll do all I can for Tee Beau and Doucette."

"Sure, you will," Fix said. "We all will. But now her husband, his papa, your brother, lay dead on a cold slab in Bayonne, and we do nothing but sit here and talk. Well, Gi-bear?"

Gil lowered his head, and didn't answer.

"I wait, I wait. I wait for all my sons, but especially for you. The one we sent to LSU. The only one in the family to ever go to LSU. The only one to ever get a high education. The educated one, Alfonze, A-goose. We wait for Mr. Educated

All-American. What does he say? He says don't move. He says sit, weep with the women. Because he wishes to be an All-American. The other one I can understand. He must sell his hog guts. He never was bright. An elementary education was his schooling. But this one—all the way to the university."

"We're doing nothing here but wasting time, Fix," Luke Will said again. "Mapes needs help."

"I won't go without my sons," Fix said. "All my sons. There will be no split in this family. This is family. Family. The majority, or none."

"And let those niggers stand there with guns, and we don't accommodate them? They want war, let's give them war," Luke Will said.

A couple of the other men agreed with him.

"I'm not interested in your war, Luke Will," Fix told him. "I'm interested only in my family. If the majority feels their brother is not worth it, then the family has spoken. I'm only interested in my family."

Gil raised his head to look at his father. He was crying.

"I'm sorry, Papa," he said.

"Sorry, Gi-bear? About what, Gi-bear?"

"Everything."

"No. Explain, Gi-bear."

"For what happened, Papa. For Beau. For us all. That you think I've gone against you, I'm sorry. I'm sorry for those old men at Marshall. Yes, Papa, I'm sorry for them, too."

"A regular Christ," Fix said. He made the sign of the cross. "A regular Christ in our midst, Alfonze, A-goose. Feels sorry for the entire world."

The two old men, very thin, sat as erect as boards, and remained quiet.

Fix continued to look at Gil. Then his head began moving back and forth, back and forth, so slightly, though, that it was almost unnoticeable. The longer he looked at Gil, the more his head moved back and forth. His dark pig eyes narrowed to where they were almost closed. He was still looking at Gil, looking at him as though all trust and belief and hope had vanished. Now he jerked his head toward him.

"Leave, Gi-bear," he said. "Go on. That is your mon's bed you sit on. Where you were born, where Beau was born, where all you were born. Now you desecrate the bed with your body upon it. Go block. Go run the ball. Let it take the place of family. Let it bring flowers to that cemetery, La Toussaint. I don't wish to see you in this house, or at that cemetery. Go. Go run the ball."

Gil could not believe what he was hearing. None of us could. He stared at his father, wanting to say something, but he could not. Fix's small dark eyes in his broad, sunburnt face assured Gil that he meant every word he spoke.

"Fix." The old man nearest him leaned forward and touched him on the arm. "Fix," he said.

"I'm dead, Alfonze," Fix said. "The one we worked for, hoped for, sacrificed for. I may as well go lay beside Maltilde."

"You're not dead, Fix," the old man said.

"They say I am—the All-American and the butcher. They say my ideas are all past. They say to love family, to defend family honor, is all past. What is left? All my life, that is all I found worthwhile living for. My family. My family. No, there's only one place left to go now, to the cemetery there in Bayonne—Beau and me beside Matilde."

"I'll go to Marshall with you, Fix," the old man said. His face did not show much emotion, and the long bony finger touching Fix's arm did not show too much life, either. "I'll take my gun and I'll go with you, if that is your wish," he said.

"Two old men, Alfonze? A-goose was right. That is a farce."

"Others will join us, I'm sure. Goudeau will join us—he

has fire in him still. Montemare, Felix Richard—Anatole will get out of that chair."

"This is family, Alfonze," Fix told him. "I have no other cause to fight for. I'm too old for causes. Let Luke Will fight for causes. This is family. A member of the family has been insulted, and family, the family must seek justice. But these, they say no. They say it is past when man must live for his family. So what else is left but to go lay in that cemetery with Beau and Matilde?" He looked at Gil sitting on the bed. "I told you to leave. Take your brother Mr. Hog Gut with you. I don't wish to see either one of you ever again. Go, change your name if that will help you be All-American. Get out of my house. Go tell your friend Mapes this old Cajun will come to Bayonne at the law's convenience. Now I have no more to say."

He took a big red print handkerchief from his back pocket and blew his nose. He put the handkerchief back and held the little boy close to his chest and looked down at the floor.

Gil stood up and turned to his brother Claude. Claude was scraping one of his thumbnails with the little pearl-handled knife.

"Claude?" Gil pleaded with him. "Claude?"

Claude went on scraping his thumbnail without answering Gil. He wouldn't even raise his head. Gil turned to one of the old men, old Alfonze. "Parrain," he said. "Haven't I been a good boy, Parrain? Haven't I always obeyed my father and obeyed you? When I come here to visit my father, don't I visit you and all the rest of the people on the bayou? Don't I go to mass with the family? Don't I get tickets so all of you can attend the games? Don't I, Parrain?" The old man looked at Fix, not at Gil. "Monsieur Auguste," Gil said to the other old man. "Aren't I a good boy, Monsieur Auguste?" But the old man only stared across the room. "Doucette?" Gil said to the woman on the bed. "You don't like me anymore, Doucette? You don't want Tee Beau to be like me anymore, Doucette? Hanh, Doucette?" The woman kept her head down and did not answer him. Gil looked around the room. The only people to look back at him were Luke Will and the other rough-looking guy, and they were not friendly looks, not by a long shot.

Gil turned back to Fix. Fix sat in the chair, head bowed, slumped a little forward, like a stone bear.

"Beat me if you want to," Gil said. "I'll get the whip. Beat me if you want to, but don't send me away from this house. Don't send me away from home, Papa?"

Fix sat there like stone. He was not hearing anything anymore.

Russ put his arm around Gil's shoulders and let him out of the room, with me a step behind them. The people in the other room had already heard what had happened, and they were not looking at Gil the way they did when he first came there. They gave him plenty of room to pass this time, and I saw a woman holding back the same little girl who had spoken to him before and wanted to come to him again. The little girl struggled and struggled, but the woman held her back, pressing the girl's head against her thigh.

We pushed our way out onto the porch. Through the screen, I could see the sun going down behind the trees on the other side of the bayou. A thin purple cloud lay across the sun, making the sky look like a nice, serene painting.

"You had to do what you did," Russ said.

"I could have run the other way," Gil said.

"And that would have been better?" Russ asked him.

"It couldn't be any worse," Gil said.

While we stood out on the porch, Luke Will and that other rough-looking guy came out there.

"If you think this is the end of it, you're crazy," Luke Will said to Gil.

"Get out of here, Luke Will," Russ said. "You don't speak for this family."

"Somebody better do it," Luke Will said.

"Nobody voted for you," Russ said.

"Maybe I'll just take it as my duty, on principle," Luke Will said.

"I don't want no trouble out of you, Luke Will," Russ said. "Stay away from Marshall, and stay out Bayonne. I'm warning you."

"You don't scare me, Russell," Luke Will said. "You or that fat belly of a boss you got there don't scare me the least."

"Just don't start any trouble," Russ said. "I'm warning you."

"The trouble already been started," Luke Will said. "When niggers start shooting down white men in broad daylight, the trouble was started then."

"We don't need your kind to settle it."

"Somebody got to do it 'fore it gets out of hand," Luke Will said. "Next thing you know, they'll be raping the women."

"That's how it is," Russ said to me. "If they can't get you one way, they'll bring in the women every time."

"Maybe you don't mind if they rape your wife or your little daughter," Luke Will said. "Maybe something like that's been going on all the time, and you just don't care."

He grinned at Russ. He wanted Russ to take a swing at him. But Russ was too cool for that.

"You see the psychology behind it all?" he said to me.

But I kept my mouth shut. I wasn't going to say a word while those two were standing there. I wasn't going to even breathe out of my mouth.

"You and your kind, your time has passed, Luke Will," Russ said.

"It ain't my time you better worry about," Luke Will said.

"I'll be around when you and your kind are long gone. You might kill him off in there," he said to Gil. "But I'm go'n be around. Let's go, Sharp."

They let the screen door slam behind them. They were both big men, big country red-necks, the kind Bull Connor used as his deputies back there in the '6os. They went across the road to a white pickup, which had a gun rack in the cab and two guns on the rack. The truck also had a CB radio, and Luke Will got on the radio and began talking. The other guy, Sharp, started up the truck and drove away. We watched it go down the road.

"What are you going to do?" Russ asked Gil.

"I don't know," Gil said.

"You want my opinion?" Russ said. "Go on back to Baton Rouge, try to get yourself some rest, play football tomorrow. Play the best game you ever played in your life."

Gil looked at Russ as if he couldn't believe what he had heard him say.

"What?" he said. "My brother is dead. Papa in there hating me, Claude hating me, Doucette, Tee Beau hating me—and you talk about a football game? Are you crazy?"

"There isn't a thing you can do here tonight," Russ said. "Tomorrow you can do something for yourself, and for all the rest of us—play the best game you ever played. Luke Will and his kind don't want to see you and Pepper in that backfield tomorrow. He doesn't ever want to see you and Pepper together."

"And what about my brother?" Gil asked. "Claude? Papa? Doucette and Tee Beau? How would it look to them?"

Russ shrugged his shoulders and shook his head. "A lot wouldn't understand. Many would hate it. But that game is going to be seen on TV by millions, and more of them will be pulling for you and Pepper than pulling against you."

"Damn the public," Gil said. "I'm talking about my family. Not the damned public. My family."

"I'm thinking about your family, too," Russ said. "Especially Tee Beau."

"And Papa?" Gil asked Russ.

"Tee Beau," Russ told him. "Tee Beau. Tee Beau's future. You want to do something for your dead brother? Do something for his son's future—play in that game tomorrow. Whether you win against Ole Miss or not, you'll beat Luke Will. Because if you don't, he'll win tomorrow, and if he does, he may just keep on winning. That's not much of a future for Tee Beau, is it?"

"What about my papa?" Gil asked. "I've already killed him. Bury him tomorrow?"

Russ laid his hand on Gil's shoulder.

"Gilly," he said. "Sometimes you got to hurt something to help something. Sometimes you have to plow under one thing in order for something else to grow. You can help Tee Beau tomorrow. You can help this country tomorrow. You can help yourself."

Gil looked away from him.

"Well," Russ said. "No more speeches. I have to report to Mapes. I'll be out there in the car if you want to talk."

He left the porch, loosening his tie. Halfway to the road, he had already taken off the tie and the coat. He hung them on a hanger in the back seat of the car; then he got in front to speak on the radio.

"He is right, Gil," I said. "We ought to go back."

Gil didn't answer me. He was looking across the road toward the trees along the bayou. The sun had sunk a little below the thin layer of purple cloud.

"What you say, Gil?"

"Leave me alone," he said. "I just want to think. Dammit, don't you see I just want to think?"

Jacques Thibeaux

aka

Tee Jack

He comes in just before sundown every day for his two Jack Daniels on the rocks. He talks sometimes; most times he's quiet and moody. The rest of the customers, no matter how long they've known him, won't start a conversation unless he speaks first. He has his own place, in the corner by the cigarette machine. From that corner he can look at the door where the nigger room used to be. He took that spot years ago so he could tell when one of his niggers came into the nigger room, and he would nod for me to go serve him something—beer, wine, whatever he wanted. Well, the nigger room's been closed now some fifteen, seventeen years. Happened when all that desegregation crap was going on—niggers didn't want to be segregated no more, so they stopped going in there. They would come to the store now and get their bottle and go squat against the wall outside to drink it, but they wouldn't go into their own little private room no more. And surely they wouldn't come in here round my white customers. Oh, once or twice, couple of them got up the nerve to try it, but from the way my white customers looked at them, and from the way I served them (shoving them their drinks and slopping some on the bar), they soon found out they wasn't welcomed. So they quit trying to desegregate the white drinking room, and just bought their bottle out of the store, and went outside or in their cars or took the bottle back home to drink it. You see, this here ain't no Marriott, and it ain't no Holiday Inn, either—not yet, and I doubt if it ever will be. This here ain't nothing but a little old bitty combination grocery store and liquor store setting in the fork of a road between a bayou and a river, where you got a room for white customers and another little private room for black customers, and that's all there is to it. When they refused, some fifteen, seventeen years ago, to come into their own little bitty room, why I just sold them their bottle from behind the counter in the grocery store and let them take it on the outside, or anywhere else they wanted to drink it, didn't make me no never mind, long as they wasn't in here bumping up against my white customers. You can call me anything you want, but that's how things are in little places like this. This ain't no Baton Rouge and it ain't no New Orleans, and it ain't no Marriott and it ain't no Holiday Inn—not yet, and God I doubt if it ever will be. Say what you want, I don't care.

But he still looks that way, toward the nigger room, each day when he comes in for his two bourbons on the rocks. Like I said, the place been closed down these past fifteen, maybe even seventeen years, and I'm using the room now for my stockroom, but he still looks there when he's drinking. Anything could be on television—football, baseball, basketball, Jap volleyball, Chinaman Ping-Pong, niggers and white boys running all over the place, nigger fags and white fags throwing little white pom-pom girls up in the air—anything. Still he looks toward that door. I wonder if he's hearing ghosts in there. I wonder if he's hearing singing coming out of there.

Sometimes when I'm here by myself, I cock my ear that way to listen, but I never hear nothing. A rat, maybe, trying to get into one of them croker sacks or one of them bags I got stacked in there, but that's about all.

You know, I sympathize with him. 'Cause you see he never wanted none of this. Never wanted to be responsible for name and land. They dropped it on him, left it on him. That's why he drinks the way he does, and let that niece of his run the place. Let her have it, he don't care. Don't care if it go to hell. He want it to go to hell. To hell with it. He go by the name 'cause they gived him that name, he live on the land 'cause they left it there, but he don't give a damn for it. That's why he drinks the way he does. Get up and drink. Take a little nap, wake up and drink some more. Take another little nap, wake up and come here. Like clockwork. Don't give a damn for nothing. Women or nothing. Pussy or nothing. Politics or nothing. Nigger or nothing. Buy them a drink 'cause Nate or Dan or Brother, one of them, left it in a will to buy it. But he don't give a damn. And I don't blame him. Things just too complicated. I reckon for people like him they have always been complicated—protecting name and land. It's just too much for most people. Feeling guilty about this, guilty about that. It wasn't his doing. He came here and found it, and they died and left it on him. You know, something just struck me. Maybe that's what he's doing when he looks at that door— cussing them. No, not the niggers who used to be in there singing—the ones who brought them here, the ones built that room. Yes, that just right this moment struck me—he's cussing them out when he's standing there gazing at that door. Sometimes he even miss his mouth with that glass, for looking at that door.

I had two other customers in the bar when he came in, and me and one of the customers had been talking about the killing. When Jack came in the door, I nodded to my customer to lower his voice. We weren't suppose to know about it yet. But something like that can't stay hidden long in a place like this. When that nigger Charlie didn't show up at the mill with them two trailers of cane at one-thirty like he was supposed to, Robert Jarreau, foreman there at Morgan, waited till round two-fifteen before he called to find out what was the matter.

Wait—hold it—let me tell you how that worked now. Beau delivered six trailers of cane to the mill six days a week during grinding. Or I should say his nigger Charlie did. The first load, two trailers each time, came in around nine, nine-thirty. The second load was ready by noon, but Beau always let Charlie eat dinner before delivering it; then after he had eaten, he would then get the second load of two trailers to the mill by one-thirty, quarter to two, depending on traffic from other trucks and tractors, of course. After delivering that load, then he would go back for the third load, which he would deliver around four, maybe four-thirty, depending on the traffic again. So when Robert didn't see that middle load come in, that one-thirty, quarter-to-two load, he waited till two-fifteen, two-thirty, then he called Fix's house to ask why. That's when they told him what had happened. Robert came over to the store around three o'clock and told me. After he had himself couple beers, he left for the mill again. For the rest of the day I waited and waited for the action. Me and one of my customers got to talking about it, and he told me where he came from—he was from Mississippi. He said folks there knowed how to take care little matters like these. I told him we had some folks right here in St. Raphael Parish who wasn't too bad at it either. I had another customer at the bar, a sallow, thoughtful-looking fellow, but he stayed quiet. Even stood a good distance away from me and the fellow from Mississippi. Didn't make me no never mind, and didn't seem to worry the Mississippi fellow either. We just went right on talking like he wasn't even there. When I saw Jack coming in, I nodded to my Mississippi customer to lower his voice.

"How are you, Jack?" I said.

He nodded. Didn't say anything. Just went over to the corner, facing the door to the old nigger room. I served him his first drink, Jack Daniels on the rocks. I could see he wasn't in no mood for talking, so I went back to my Mississippi customer.

"Got to move on," he said. "Having supper with some of the boys in town. You sure you don't want to put a little bet on the game?"

"Don't like to take money from a new customer," I said.

He laughed. A pleasant fellow.

"Better pray nothing happen to Salt or Pepper," he said. "Ole Miss would run the draws off 'em."

He finished his drink and left me fifty cents tip.

"Thanks," I said. "Can't wish you good luck, 'cause you know who I'm pulling for."

He laughed and went out. A nice fellow, real nice fellow.

It was quiet after he had gone. Jack had nothing to say, and the other fellow had even less than that to talk about. I was sure he was educated, always thinking. When he needed a drink, he just nodded toward his glass. Never saying, "Say, bartender," or anything like that—just a little nod toward his empty glass. After I served him, he would nod again. Never a word. Damn if I didn't think I was in a morgue instead of a bar. Went on like that fifteen, twenty minutes—till Robert came in again. I was so glad to see him I almost offered him a free beer.

"Heard about Beau?" he asked.

Now, Robert knew Jack was in there. He had already seen Jack's car before the door, and he knew Jack came to my place around this time every day God send. But I wasn't supposed to know what had happened, not yet.

"What about Beau?" I said.

"Got himself killed," Robert said. "Oh, hello, Jack," he said to Marshall.

Marshall nodded. Didn't say anything.

"Beau killed?" I said. "How did it happen? Where? When?"

I'm a pretty good actor when I want to be.

"On that plantation," Robert said, glancing at Jack. "Bring me a Miller," he said to me.

"Jack, that's true?" I asked Marshall.

He nodded.

I got the Miller for Robert. Me and Robert looked at each other. He was a pretty good actor himself, there.

"Murder?" I asked Robert.

"Mapes over there now questioning niggers," Robert said. "Hilly told me."

"Boy, boy, boy, we haven't had a good stringing in these parts in quite a while," I said. "We'll have one now, if you know Fix."

"That kind of thing is over with," the quiet customer said.

I almost jumped. It was like if a dead man had just spoke. That was the most he had said since ordering his first drink. Me and Robert looked down the bar at him, but didn't answer him. Jack never looked up from his drink.

"When did it happen?" I asked Robert.

"Dinnertime," Robert said.

"And Fix ain't here yet?"

"Not yet," Robert said.

"He'll be here," I said. "You can bet your boots old Fix will ride before this night is over with."

"That kind of thing doesn't happen anymore," the quiet customer said again. He didn't look at us when he spoke. He was looking in the mirror behind the bar. Then he turned to Jack. "Don't you agree, Mister? That kind of thing doesn't happen anymore?"

Jack didn't look at him for a while; then he looked at him a time before answering. He didn't like for anybody to ask him a question uninvited.

"I don't think we've progressed that much yet," he said, looking at the door, not at the customer. I wondered if he heard ghosts singing in there.

"I was hoping we had progressed some," the quiet customer said quietly.

He looked at Jack a long time. Jack, in his neat gray suit, white shirt, and tie, looked like an intelligent man. The kind of man another man could have an intelligent conversation with. But Jack wasn't interested. He didn't look at the customer when he answered him, and he surely wasn't looking at him now. He was looking down at his drink.

Robert was drinking a Miller's beer a good heavy man's width from Jack Marshall. Nobody got much closer than that to Jack, unless it was Felix Morgan, no matter how crowded the place got. Though he came here to drink, sometimes even bought a round, he would let you know he was not of your crowd. Felix Morgan was. The Morgan family owned the joining plantation and the sugar mill where most of the cane in this parish was ground.

I had just poured Jack his second drink when Luke Will, Sharp Thompson, Henry Tobias, Alcee Boudreaux, and that boy Leroy Hall came in. They came in the place once or twice a week. I had kinda expected to see them tonight, and still I had kinda not expected to see them so soon again, since I had just seen Luke Will, Sharp Thompson, and Beau together the night before. So I was a little surprised, but maybe not too surprised, not after what had happened.

"Gentlemen," Luke Will said, in that big, hoarse voice he's got there.

Luke Will and Sharp Thompson were truck drivers for the Dixie Gravel, Cement & Dirt Company of Bayonne. The other three with them worked for the same company. On the side, they did other little jobs to keep things running smoothly in the parish. Like turning over nigger school buses, throwing a few snakes into nigger churches during prayer meetings, or running niggers out of what used to be all-white motels and restaurants. Some people say they got paid as much for these little civic duties as they did at that dirt plant. But nobody knew where the money was coming from, or if they did know, they knew better than to go blabbing about it.

"Boys," I said. "Nice day, isn't it?"

They pushed their way up to the bar. They stood at the opposite end of the bar from Jack Marshall. Robert and the other customer was between them and Jack. Jack was looking down at his drink. If he raised his head, he would see Luke Will, not the door to the old nigger room. Luke Will was about the same size as the door.

"Give us a bottle, Tee Jack," Luke Will said. "Bring some Cokes."

"No beer tonight, boys?" I asked.

"Just bring a bottle," Luke Will said, and looked down the bar at Jack. "Mr. Marshall, how are you?" he said.

Jack Marshall looked toward Luke Will and nodded.

"Had some trouble, I hear?" Luke Will said.

"I didn't have any," Jack said, not looking at him, just looking that way.

"That thing with Beau," Luke Will said.

"I heard he got himself killed," Jack said, with no more feeling than if somebody had told him a rat was dead.

"One of your niggers did it, Mr. Marshall," Luke Will said.

Jack Marshall looked at him now. He wasn't just looking in that direction; he was looking straight at him.

"I have no niggers," he said. "Never had any niggers. Never wanted any niggers. Never will have any niggers. They belong to her."

"Where is Candy?" Luke Will asked.

"In the quarters, I should think."

"Protecting her niggers?"

"I have no idea what she's doing."

"Is Mapes still down there playing detective?"

"From what I hear he is," Jack said. "Now, if you don't mind, I would like to finish my drink."

"Another second of your time, Mr. Marshall," Luke Will said.

Jack Marshall had already looked down. Since he couldn't see the door anymore, he thought he might's well look down at his glass. He didn't raise his head. I reckon he had already talked to Luke Will and his kind more than he had ever done at any one time before. I started to tell Luke Will to lay off, but then I said to myself, "Oh, what the hell. Jack Marshall don't own my place, I do. And the only reason he comes here, it's the nearest saloon to his fancy house there on the river." Jack looked up.

"I think Mapes needs help," Luke Will said.

Jack looked at him, but with no more feeling than if he was looking at a chinaball tree or a fence post. He showed more concern looking at that door to the nigger room than he did looking at a live Luke Will.

"I hope you wouldn't mind," Luke Will said.

"Are you suggesting I go down there and help him?" Jack asked.

"Not exactly," Luke Will said.

"What are you suggesting?" Jack asked.

Luke Will and his boys, all five of them, looked at Jack. We all knowed what Luke Will was suggesting. Jack did, too. Luke Will didn't say any more. Nobody did. And I went on serving. I set a bottle of Old Crow, glasses, Cokes, and a bowl of ice on the bar. Luke Will and his boys started digging their hands into the ice bowl, and pouring their own drinks. I glanced into the ice bowl, and I could see dirt and grit settled at the bottom. Couple of these boys had not washed their hands since leaving work.

"Law seems to work slow at times," the quiet customer said quietly. "But it's still the best thing that we have. Was it Churchill who said that?" He took out a pipe. "You gentlemen don't mind, do you?"

Nobody answered him. He lit the pipe.

Luke Will turned up the glass, and half the drink was gone. When he turned it up again, everything was gone except the ice, and he fixed himself another drink.

"The old man ain't showing up," he said.

"What?" I said.

"His All-American son talked him out of it," Luke Will said.

"That's a lie," I said.

Luke Will and his boys looked at me all at the same time.

"What's that you said, Tee Jack?" Luke Will asked.

"I didn't mean it," I said. "God in Heaven knows I didn't mean that. Just slipped out, just slipped out, hearing that Fix wasn't coming here tonight. Just slipped out."

"Be careful, Tee Jack, my fuse is short," Luke Will said.

"I can see why," I said. "I can see why. Listen, why don't you boys just have that bottle on me? Show you where my heart at. Don't have to pay me a penny. Have it on me. All right?"

They all said all right, and I felt a little better. I had thought about that Little League baseball bat under the bar. I knew I couldn't do much with it against all five of them, but you got to use what you got.

"I think it's the right thing to do," the man with the pipe said.

Now, why did he have to go and open his mouth just when things was settling down? He didn't even know these boys. I knew them, and he could see they were ready to jump across that bar on me, so what chance would he have? They would lynch him like they would a nigger, that's what.

"What's that you said, Mister?" Luke Will asked him.

"Let the law handle this," the pipe man said, not even looking at Luke Will.

"Say, where you from, Mister?" Leroy asked. "Not one of them New York Yankee NAPC Jews, are you?"

The fellow took the pipe from his mouth and looked at Leroy. Leroy was no more than seventeen, eighteen at the most. I wasn't supposed to let him drink in here, but I wasn't no fool, not with that crowd.

"Texas," the pipe man said. "Teaching at USL. Lafayette."

"What you teaching there, nigger study?" Leroy asked.

"I teach black writing, among other things," the man from USL said. He held the stem of his pipe against the corner of his mouth while he looked at Leroy. Looked like he was trying to figure out what Leroy was. You know how you look at a headless and gutted animal in a butcher shop, and for a while you don't know exactly what it is? Well, that's the way that schoolteaching fellow was looking at Leroy.

"Ain't you a little late for class?" Leroy asked him.

"None on Friday nights," the fellow said.

"You must have one. Think, now," Leroy said.

The pipe man thought for a couple of seconds; then he shook his head. "Nope. None that I can recall," he said.

"Then why don't you just go on back to Lafayette and start up one," Leroy said, stepping a little closer to the fellow from USL.

"Now, now, Leroy," I said. "Calm down, calm down."

"Sure," Leroy said, looking at the fellow. "Sure."

He finished his drink, and went back and fixed up another one. I looked at that pipe fellow from USL. I hate putting a white man out of my place, but I sure wished that fellow would go on home.

"So Fix's leaving it up to Mapes, huh?" Robert asked Luke Will. He raised the empty bottle for me to bring him another Miller.

"It's not him," Luke Will said to Robert. "It's that All-American fart and that hog-gut salesman there in Bayonne. They the ones talked him out of it. He wanted to come, but he wouldn't come without them. I left him there crying."

"My God," I said. I served Robert, and collected my money. "What is this world coming to?" I said. "What in the world is this world coming to?"

Jack finished his drink and set the glass on the bar.

"Good night," he said, moving out of the corner.

"Leaving us, Jack?"

"Yes."

Jack had to pass by Robert and that fellow from USL to reach the door, and that schoolteaching fellow turned from the bar to look at him.

"Sir?" he said. "Don't you own that place?"

Jack stopped and looked at the fellow. He didn't like for strangers to speak to him unless he spoke first.

"What place?" he asked.

"Where Beau was killed."

"I own a third of it," Jack said.

"Don't you think you ought to do something?"

"The law is down there," Jack said. "That's what they pay him for."

"I mean something else," the man from USL said.

"What?" Jack said.

That fellow just looked at Jack. Jack looked right back at him, but not showing a thing in his face.

"Sir, you seem like an intelligent man," that fellow said.

"Sure," Jack said. "So what?"

"You must care something for the place, for the people who live there?"

"They live pretty well," Jack said. "They don't pay rent or anything."

"And what's happening here now, that doesn't matter?"

"I don't see anything happening," Jack said. "Do you?"

That fellow just looked at Jack. He couldn't believe Jack. But he didn't know Jack, either.

"In the end, it's people like us, you and I, who pay for this."

"Sure," Jack said. "But I've been paying my share seventy years already. How long have you been paying yours?"

"The debt is never finished as long as we stand for this," the teacher said.

Jack grunted. No change, though, no change in his face at all. "If you can't take it here, you better get on back to Texas," he said, and went out.

He backed the car from in front of the door, and drove on up the river. The shadows from the trees on the riverbank covered everything now. Soon it would be dark—and Luke Will and his boys were putting that liquor away faster and faster.

"He sure cooked your goose," Leroy told the fellow from USL.

The teacher didn't look at Leroy. He was looking in the mirror behind the bar. Leroy was getting drunk. His young childish face had turned beet red. His blue eyes had gotten bluer. His small reddish lips shoulda been on a girl, not a man.

"Bring us another bottle there, Tee Jack," Luke Will said.

'Sure, boys, sure," I said. "Remember, now, the first one was on me." The way I said *first,* I wanted them to know that this one was not on me. I didn't think I had insulted him two bottles' worth when I called him a liar.

I set up the bar, and they dug in. I took a quick little peek into the ice bowl again. Yep, dirt and grit covered the bottom. Some of these boys hadn't seen a washbasin in weeks.

"You down there," Luke Will said to the teacher from USL. "Don't you think you ought to get moving?"

"I was just thinking about it," the fellow said.

"Don't think," Luke Will said. "Move it."

The fellow knocked some ashes out of his pipe into the palm of his hand; then he dumped the ashes into the little tin ashtray I had on the bar.

"You boys think you're doing the right thing, taking the law in your own hands?"

"You leaving, or you need some escorting?" Luke Will asked him.

"I'm leaving," the teacher said. "But I will leave with these parting words. Don't do it. For the sake of the South. For Salt and Pepper, don't do it."

"Sharp, you and Henry show that gentleman to his car," Luke Will said. "If he don't have one, start him walking toward Lafayette."

"Luke, please," I said. "He's a white man. That can make trouble."

"If he's a white man, let him act like one," Luke Will said. "Sharp, you and Henry."

Sharp Thompson and Henry Tobias started toward the teacher from USL. That teacher raised his hands quick.

"I'm leaving," he said.

"You better go straight to Lafayette, too," Luke Will said. "I know how to find that schoolhouse. I cross that Atchafalaya Basin every day."

The teacher looked at Robert, but Robert looked down at his bottle of beer. The teacher looked at me, but he could see I wasn't on his side either. I wasn't against him, but he was a stranger here, and these were my regular customers—and I wasn't no fool either. I didn't want to come in here one day and find a bunch of rattlesnakes and water moggassins crawling all over the place.

That poor fellow couldn't find anybody to go along with

him, and he nodded to himself and went out. You never in all your born days seen a sadder-looking figure. Fellow acted like he carried the whole world on his shoulders all by himself.

"You ought to mind who you let come in your place, Tee Jack," Luke Will said to me.

"How can you tell a book by the cover?" I said. "He looked all right when he first came in. A little on the weak, worrying side, but he looked all right."

"Be more careful in the future," Luke Will said.

"Sure," I said. "You know me. Anything to please my regular customers."

"One more, and I'm ready to kick me some ass," Leroy said, fixing another drink. "Shit, I can't wait. Let's go kick some ass."

"Take it easy, boy," Luke Will said. "You'll get your chance."

"I close at ten on Fridays, boys," I said. "The old lady, you know."

"Tonight you'll stay open long as we want you to," Luke Will said.

"Sure, boys, sure," I said. I thought about all them rattlesnakes and moggassins crawling all over the place. "Anything to please my regular customers." I looked across the bar at Robert. He was just finishing his beer. He had already glanced over his shoulder toward the door. "Like another one?" I asked him. I wanted him to stay there with me. Lord, I *needed* him to stay there with me. "On the house this time," I said. "On the house."

"No, I'm going home," Robert said. "I haven't been here at all today. Good night."

"It's on the house," I said. "Any kind you like. Two of any brand."

He went out. I heard him get in his car and drive away. I didn't look around at Luke Will and his boys. I faced the empty end of the bar, scared and feeling all alone. Nobody said anything. I could feel they was enjoying my fear.

"Look at him, look at him," I heard Leroy saying. "Shaking there like a scared old nigger. Now you know how a old nigger feel. Look at him, look at him."

I wouldn't look around, so he moved down the bar to face me. He started pointing his finger and laughing at me. He was drunk now, drunk as he could be, and his soft, girlish face and little red, girlish lips made him look like a freak I had once seen at a carnival show.

"Let's finish this bottle and get out of here," Luke Will said.

Albert Jackson

a k a

Rooster

After Miss Merle left with her two baskets, Lou went out in the road where Mapes was. They leaned back against Mapes's car looking at us in the yard. Me, I was leaning back against the end of the garry where you went around the house to the toilet. Chimley had just come from the toilet, and before he got back to the front I seen him bending over and getting a shell out of the shoe box under the house. He got two. He put one in the gun, the other one in his pocket. You see, that's what we had been doing all the time. Sure, we was going back to the toilet, but we was doing more than just going to the toilet. Clatoo had already told us where he had put that box of shells, and every time one of us went to the toilet, and didn't catch the white folks watching us, we ducked down by the side of the house and got a couple shells out of that box. And nobody knowed the difference. Not my wife, Beulah, not none of the other women, and surely not that crazy Jameson. We was more scared of him talking than we was anybody else.

Not long after Chimley had come back to the front, we heard the noise on the car radio. Mapes opened the door and started talking on the speaker. We could hear the static, then the other voice; the static, then Mapes. It went on like that couple minutes—static, other voice; static, then Mapes. Then he hung up the speaker, and him and Lou came back in the yard. Mapes was grinning. Oh, how he was grinning. Not grinning out, grinning in. You could tell he was grinning in, even if his mouth wasn't moving.

"All right, gather round here," he said.

The people moved in slowly. It had been a long day. The sun was just about down. Mosquitoes was already coming out of the weeds. Everybody was tired, but nobody was thinking about going home—not yet. Not till this was settled and over with.

"Look like you boys put on your brave hats just a little too late," Mapes said. "Fix ain't showing up."

He grinned. His big old jaws was all puffed out. He looked all around, grinning. But nobody was grinning back, because nobody wanted to believe him. We had put in too much to have this day end like this.

Johnny Paul spoke first. "That's a lie," he said.

Johnny Paul wasn't standing more than a arm reach from Mapes. But Mapes didn't want to hit him. He felt grinning at Johnny Paul was good enough. He could arrest Johnny Paul and beat him anytime. Right now, grinning at Johnny Paul was good enough.

"I say that's a lie," Johnny Paul said to the rest of us. "Just trying to make us go home. Y'all know Fix. You know he got to show up."

We all said we knowed Fix and Fix had to show up.

"Hah," Mapes said, grinning.

"That's just to throw us off," Johnny Paul said. "Another white man trick. Look at the blood on that grass. That's Fix boy's blood. You think Fix ain't go show up—his own blood on that grass?"

"He got to show up," Mat said.

"You darn right he got to show up," Johnny Paul said. "Look at the spot on that grass."

We all looked at the spot where Beau had fell. The grass was mashed down, the blood still there.

"He still ain't showing up," Mapes said. "So y'all might's well go on home."

"The sheriff lying," Johnny Paul said to the rest of us. He turned back to Mapes. "Come on, Sheriff, I called you a lie right in front of a bunch of niggers. Ain't you go'n take me in?"

Mapes shook his head. He pointed his finger at Johnny Paul.

"You're trying to be a hero today, Johnny Paul, and you want me to help you. Well, I ain't."

The rest of us stood there looking at Mapes. We didn't know what to do. We didn't want to believe him even if he was telling the truth. We had cranked usself up for a fight, and we wanted usself a fight.

"That just don't sound like Fix," Clatoo said, from the garry. "Nothing could keep Fix from Marshall today."

"That's where you're wrong, Mr. Clatoo," Mapes said, going up closer to the garry and looking up at Clatoo. "Now, that's what I thought, too. Because, you see, me, you, and all the rest of them were thinking about Fix thirty years ago. Thirty years ago Fix woulda been here, woulda hanged Mathu on the nearest tree, and all the rest of you brave people woulda been still hiding under the bed. But something happened the last ten, fifteen years. Salt and Pepper got together. Now, it's nobody's fault but yours," Mapes said, looking round at all of us. "Nobody's fault but yours. Y'all did it. Y'all wasn't satisfied Salt played at LSU on one side of town, and Pepper played for Southern on the other side of town— no, y'all wanted them to play together. Y'all prayed and prayed and prayed for them to play together. Well, they did—and that's what happened. Salt went back and talked to his daddy. Gil—that white boy who stopped by here—that's Salt. Y'all know him, you seen him on television enough. Went back and told his daddy he needed Pepper and Pepper needed him. Told his daddy he wouldn't go along with his daddy to lynch Mathu. Told his daddy, even, if the name Boutan got in the papers, he would never be All-American. But y'all the ones did it," Mapes said. He was moving around the yard. He was looking us all in the face. Stop a second and look at one, then move, and stop and look at another one awhile. "Y'all the one—you cut your own throats. You told God you wanted Salt and Pepper to get together, and God did it for you. At the same time, you wanted God to keep Fix the way Fix was thirty years ago so one day you would get a chance to shoot him. Well, God couldn't do both. Not that He likes Fix, but He thought the other idea was better—Salt and Pepper. Well? Which do you want? Salt and Pepper to play together, or you want God to keep Fix the way he was thirty years ago so you would have a chance to shoot him? Well, make up your mind. I'm sure God's just sitting there waiting."

We all thought Mapes had gone crazy. But it turned out he was just happy. I had never seen a happier white man in all my born days. Looked like he was ready to kiss the first person who come up.

"Well, ain't somebody go'n say something?" he said, looking around.

We didn't know what to say. We didn't know where to turn. It was quiet. Quiet, quiet. You couldn't hear a sound no matter how hard you listened. No moving. Nothing. Quiet.

Mapes turned to Mathu, sitting there on the end of the step.

"Ready, old sport?"

"I'm ready," Mathu said.

Candy had been standing next to Mathu all this time. Even when Mapes passed right by her, talking, she never paid him any mind. I don't know if she was even hearing him. She didn't show it, until he mentioned Mathu's name; then she went out to the walk. Easy like that, she just went out to the walk and stood there with her arms folded.

"What you think you doing?" Mapes asked her. "Don't you know when the show is over?"

Candy didn't answer him. Then my wife left the steps and joined Candy on the walk. I joined my wife. Then everybody started joining in. Glo and her three little grandchildren. Even Corrine managed to get down the steps and come out in the yard.

Mapes was looking at us. He had Mathu by the arm with one hand; he had his gun in the other hand.

"I said the show was over with," he said. "Don't make me hurt anybody."

Nobody moved.

"Clear off that walk, Griffin," Mapes said. "I'm not walking around anybody. Use that gun if you have to."

Griffin had been standing over by the garden with the gun stuck in his belt. He took it out and started toward us. Mat, Cherry Bello, one of the Lejeune brothers raised their guns. Not high. Belt-level.

Griffin stopped.

"Hold it," Clatoo said, from the garry. "Hold it. Sheriff, can we talk? Can me and the rest of the men talk to Mathu inside?"

Mapes was still looking at us. Griffin was looking at us too. He didn't know if them guns was loaded or not, and he wasn't taking any chance.

Mapes looked back at Clatoo. "Talk?" he said. "Talk about what? All I heard since I've been here was talk."

"Give us a couple minutes," Clatoo said. "You can spare us that."

Mapes looked back at us on the walk. More of us had raised our guns belt-level.

"All right," Mapes said to Clatoo. "You have a couple minutes. Make it quick. I'm tired now."

"Y'all come on inside," Clatoo said to us. "Not you, Candy," he said to her.

"Nobody's talking without me," Candy said, coming back toward the garry.

"This time we have to, Candy," Clatoo said. "Just the men with guns."

"Like hell," Candy said. "This is my place."

"I know that, Candy," Clatoo said. "But we don't want you there this time."

That stopped her. Nobody talked to Candy like that—black or white—and specially not black.

"What the hell did you say?" she asked Clatoo. "You know where you're at? You know who you're talking to? Get the hell off my place."

"I'm not going anywhere, Candy," Clatoo said.

"What?" she said.

"Not till this is cleared up," Clatoo said to her. "I already told the sheriff I don't mind going to jail, or even dying today. And that means I ain't taking no orders either."

Candy was mad now. She was so mad she was trembling. She tried to make Clatoo look down, but Clatoo wouldn't look no farther down than her eyes. Now she turned to Mapes. Any other time, she wouldn't need to turn to Mapes; Mapes woulda brought Clatoo off that garry even if he had to shoot him down. But this time he just grinned at Candy. He liked what was happening; one of us talking back to her. Candy turned to Lou. Lou reached out his hand and called her name for her to come to him. She turned back on us.

"Y'all can go on and listen to Clatoo if y'all want," she said. "But remember this—Clatoo got a little piece of land to go back to. Y'all don't have nothing but this. You listen to him now, and you won't even have this."

Mapes laughed out loud. Not in now—out. "Well, well, well," he said. "Listen to the savior now. Do what she wants or you're out in the cold. Did y'all hear that?"

Candy turned on him. "You've been trying to split us up all day," she said.

"And you want to keep them slaves the rest of their lives," Mapes said back.

"Nobody is a slave here," Candy said. "I'm protecting them like I've always protected them. Like my people have always protected them. Ask them."

"At least your people let them talk," Mapes said. "That's why they put that church up there. Now you're trying to take that away from them."

Candy didn't know how to answer Mapes. So she turned on Mathu.

"Is that what you want?" she asked him. "You want to go in there alone—without me?"

Mathu shook his head. "Candy, I'm just tired," he said. "If that's what they want, it's all right with me. I just wanta get this over with."

Candy didn't say another word. Like a cat, she sprung up on the garry, went right by Clatoo, and stood in the door with her hands on her hips.

"Now, who'll go by me?" she asked.

"Come down from there," Mapes said. "They want to talk, they'll talk. You come on down from there."

Candy wasn't listening, just standing there with her hands on her hips, daring anybody.

"Griffin," Mapes said to his deputy. "Get up there and pull her away from that door."

Old Griffin still had his gun out. He made two steps toward the garry, and stopped.

"Well?" Mapes said.

"He knows I'll bust his jaw," Candy said.

"Get up them steps, Griffin," Mapes said, going on him. Griffin didn't go up the steps, but he moved away from Mapes, and Mapes was too fat to catch him. The people laughed. Mapes turned on us to make us shut up. Then he looked back at Candy. "Come down from there, Candy," he said. "If I come up them steps, you're going to jail, just sure as hell."

Candy didn't move.

"Come down, Candy," Lou told her. "Don't make a spectacle of yourself in front of these people."

"She's been doing that all day," Mapes said. "Tell her not to make a bigger ass of herself."

We all looked at Candy standing in the door with her hands on her hips. Beulah laughed out loud. "Stand your ground, honey," she said. "Just stand your ground."

"You better shut your goddamn mouth," Mapes told her. "I'm tired now. You hear me? I'm tired."

"Let me talk to her, Sheriff," Mathu said, and went up the steps.

Candy watched Mathu coming toward her. Her hands was on her hips at first; then they slid to her side, like she was ready to fight Mathu if he said the wrong thing. But as he got closer to her, you could see her face changing, you could see her fists loosening.

"I want you to go home," he said. Not loud. Quiet. Soft. The way he used to talk to her when she was a little girl.

She shook her head.

"That's what I want," he said.

She shook her head again.

Years ago, when she was five or six, she used to come down

here and play in his yard and follow him around in the garden. Near sundown he would tell her to go on home. "No," she would say. "Go on home." "No," she would say. He would take her by the hand or put her on his shoulder or on his back and ride her up to the big house. The next day, near sundown: "Go on home, now." "No," she would say.

Now they looked at each other. I could see her biting her lip. She wanted to cry. But she couldn't, not in front of us.

"I have to go," Mathu said. "I have to pay."

"No," she said. "Daddy and Grandpa said you paid enough. You always paid for them. You won't pay for me, too."

He laid his old hand against her face, and she helt it there.

Lou had followed Mathu up the steps, but he stayed back while they talked. When they got quiet, he moved in a little closer.

"Let's go, Candy," he said.

She didn't even hear him. Mathu had brought his hand down from her face, but she still helt his hand with both of hers.

"This is not Marshall, without you," she told him.

"I'll always be here, Candy," he said.

"This is nothing but a few miles of dirt," she said. "Weeds, trees, dirt—but this is not Marshall without you."

"I'll be here," he said.

"Candy," Lou said.

"You knew the first," Candy said to Mathu. She wasn't hearing Lou at all. "You knew Grandpa Nate. The first Marshall. Remember from the war—the Civil War?"

"I remember the Colonel."

"You knew them all," Candy said. "Grew up with my grandpa. Raised my daddy. Raised me. I want you to help me with my own child one day."

"I'll be here," he said.

"Not like that," she said. "Not back there under those

trees—spirit alone. I want you to hold his hand. Tell him about Grandpa. Tell him about the field. Tell him how the river looked before the cabins and wharves. No one else to tell him about these things but you."

"I'll tell him," he said.

"No," she said. "You can't tell him from the grave. You'll die if they put you in that jail. And this place'll die, too. There's no reason for this place to be if you're not here. My daddy, he said, you, you, you."

"I'll be here," he said.

"Candy," Lou said.

"Go with him," Mathu said. "It's time you went to him. I'll be all right."

Lou moved in closer. "Come on, Candy," he said.

Candy still helt Mathu's hand. "My daddy, all of them, said it was you, you, you," she said. Lou pulled on her, but she was still holding on to Mathu. "They said it was Mathu," she said. "They said Mathu. They said you were. They said it was you."

"Come on, Candy," Lou said, pulling on her.

"They said if you went, it went, because we could not—it could not—not without you, Mathu."

Mathu covered her hands with his big old ashy, gray-black hand and pulled her free. Lou picked her up, under his arm, and came with her down the steps. Candy was cussing him, hitting at him, cussing Mapes, kicking, but Lou didn't pay her any mind. He took her out to the road, throwed her into her own car, and slammed the door. Then he stood there with his back against the door, looking at us in the yard.

"Y'all got fifteen minutes," Mapes said to us. "Then I'm taking him in. If y'all want to come along, you're welcome. But I'm warning you, you follow me to Bayonne, I'm throwing the book at you for interfering with the law. Now, you got exactly fifteen minutes."

We went inside. It was dark in there, and Clatoo pulled the string to turn on the light. You could see from the way the place was kept Mathu stayed there by himself. The wallpaper his wife, Lottie, had put there years, years ago was all faded and torn. Dirtdobbers' nests hung on the wall and on the picture frames. Cobwebs hung from the ceiling. Mathu had a old chifforobe in one corner, an old washstand with a china bowl and a pitcher in another corner, a old brass bed sagging in the middle against the wall by the window, and a rocking chair and a bench by the firehalf. He had a coal-oil lamp on the mantelpiece, in case 'lectricity went out. His old tin cup he used to take out in the field was on the mantelpiece, too. The old cup was so old it had turned black. Mathu stood at one end of the firehalf, Clatoo at the other end. Billy Washington caught the door, Rufe caught the window. Now it was hot and stuffy in there with the door and window both closed.

"Well," Clatoo said. "What we go'n do? Y'all can see the man's patient done run out."

"Ain't we go'n do what we was go'n do from the start?" Johnny Paul said. Johnny Paul was standing in the back of the room with some of the others. "If Mathu go to jail, we going, too—ain't that's what we said?"

"Now, listen," Clatoo said.

"Ain't that's what we said?" Johnny Paul said, from the back of the room.

I was kinda short, so I had pushed myself up closer to the firehalf. I had Yank on one side of me, Tucker on the other side of me, and Dirty Red right behind me. Clatoo looked over all of us at Johnny Paul in the back of the room.

"Give me one minute," Clatoo said. "One minute. Now, listen. Y'all know I love this man," he said, and nodded toward Mathu. "Y'all know I'd do anything for this man. Y'all know I respect this man like I don't respect too many men. And y'all know why. He always stood up. Stood up to Fix, stood up to anybody who tried to do him wrong. Even to the Marshalls out there at the front, he stood his ground. That's why Jack Marshall don't like Mathu today, Mathu always stood up. Stood up to Jack Marshall, too. And that's why I come here today, to stand with this man. To die with him, 'side him, if I have to. That's why we all come here—out of respect for him. To fight 'side him. To fight, gentlemen. But now fight who? There ain't nobody to fight, gentlemen. Nobody to fight." Clatoo looked at all of us now. We all had our guns. All of us ready. "Gentlemen," he said. "Let's call it a day and go back home."

All of a sudden I got knocked almost in the firehalf. It was Johnny Paul pushing his way up to the front. He had pushed against Dirty Red, Dirty Red had fell against me, and I had almost fell over in the firehalf.

"Now what the hell you think you saying, Clatoo?" Johnny Paul asked him. Johnny Paul and Clatoo was about same height. They could look each other eye to eye. "What the hell we come here for if not to stand to the end?"

The rest of us went along with Johnny Paul. We all said we came to stay to the end. Clatoo picked up Mathu's old field cup and rapped it on the mantelpiece.

"Give me one more minute, one more minute, and I'll shut up if you want me to shut up," he said.

We all got quiet.

"Now, y'all heard the man," Clatoo said. "He's going to take Mathu in."

"Then we go, too," Johnny Paul said.

"Go for what, Johnny Paul?" Clatoo asked him. "Do what when we get there?"

"Same thing we was go'n do before," Johnny Paul said.

Clatoo took in a deep breath and shook his head. "Johnny Paul, that man won't even lock us up now. You know why? Because tomorrow this time he know he can prove most of us wasn't nowhere around this place. He just went along with us out there because of Fix. He didn't want us in Bayonne with these shotguns, because he didn't want Fix to come and find us there. But now Fix ain't showing up, and he ain't worried about us no more. He never took us serious, not for once. Fix was on his mind, not us. Fix, Johnny Paul."

"I don't care what was on Mapes's mind, or what's on y'all mind, but this is what's on my mind. If Mathu leave from here tonight, I'm leaving with him. We all had good reason to kill Beau."

"But we didn't do it," Clatoo said.

"Nobody can say I didn't do it," Johnny Paul said. "I got the same make gun."

"But *you* know you didn't do it, Johnny Paul," Clatoo said. "You know in your heart you didn't do it." He looked over the room. "Can't the rest of y'all understand what I'm trying to say? Jacob? Mat? Y'all understand what I'm trying to say, don't you?"

"I see your point," Mat said, from over by the door. "But we come here to stand, Clatoo. I don't feel like going back home empty-handed. We'll never gather like this ever again."

"But we've already done it, Mat," Clatoo said. "Don't you see, we've already done it? Nobody is leaving here empty-handed. We've already stood. Go to Bayonne now for what? Do what in Bayonne when we get there? March around that courthouse and sing—with loaded guns? Guns made for fighting with, but we ain't got a enemy to fight."

"I already said what I'm go'n do," Johnny Paul said. "If Mathu go to Bayonne, I go to Bayonne with him."

He pushed his way back to the back of the room.

It was quiet for a while. I was thinking how I was picking up pecans behind the quarters when my wife sent and called for me. I was thinking how scared I was when she told me I had to go find a shotgun somewhere, and how scared I was when I went up to Aunt Lena and asked her to borrow it. I was thinking now about all the hurt I had suffered, the insults my wife had suffered right in front of my face. I was thinking about what all the old people musta gone through even before me. I was thinking about all that—and this was the day we was go'n get even. But now here Clatoo was saying we ought to go back home. Go back home and do what? I hadn't even fired a shot. Just one, in that pecan tree, so I could have a empty shell. No, that wasn't enough. Not after what I had put up with all these years. I wanted me a fight, even if I had to get killed.

"There ain't no more to prove," I heard Mathu saying. "Y'all done already proved it."

I had been looking down at the floor. Now I looked up at Mathu. He leaned against the mantelpiece. He was tired, his voice weak and shaky. He looked right at me, smiling. He never thought much of me. Used to call me Little Red Rooster all the time. People even said him and Beulah had fooled around some behind my back. I never asked him, I never asked her—I was too scared. But I wasn't scared now. He knowed I wasn't scared now. That's why he was smiling at me. And that made me feel good.

"I never thought I woulda seen this day," he said. "No, I never thought I woulda seen this day. Rooster with a gun, Dirty Red with a gun—Chimley, Billy. No, I never thought I woulda seen this day."

I looked up at him, holding my gun tight to my side and feeling proud.

"Till a few minutes ago, I felt the same way that man out there feel about y'all—you never would 'mount to anything. But I was wrong. And he's still wrong. 'Cause he ain't go'n ever face the fact. But now I know. And I thank y'all. And I look up to you. Every man in here. And this the proudest day of my life."

He stopped. His voice got hoarse. Couple times his lips moved, but nothing came out. We waited. My heart was beating fast and hard. I helt my gun tight, looking up at him. No, he wasn't the proudest man in this house. I was.

"I ain't nothing but a mean, bitter old man," he said. "No hero. Lord—no hero. A mean, bitter old man. Hating them out there on that river, hating y'all here in the quarters. Put myself above all—proud to be African. You know why proud to be African? 'Cause they won't let me be a citizen here in this country. Hate them 'cause they won't let me be a citizen, hated y'all 'cause you never tried. Just a mean-hearted old man. All I ever been, till this hour."

He stopped and looked down at me again, looked at me a good while, nodding his head.

"I been changed," he said. "I been changed. Not by that white man's God. I don't believe in that white man's God. I been changed by y'all. Rooster, Clabber, Dirty Red, Coot—you changed this hardhearted old man."

He stopped again, looking across the room at the people.

"Clatoo is right, I want y'all to go home." His voice was getting hoarse again, and he had to stop and clear his throat. His lips moved, but nothing came out till he cleared his throat again. "Go home, Johnny Paul," he said. He looked at Johnny Paul a good two or three seconds; then he looked at somebody else. He would call that person's name, look at him awhile, then turn to somebody else. "Go home, Dirty Red. Aunt Jude and Unc François happy tonight." Then to somebody else for two or three seconds. "Go home, Rufe. Go home, Yank, Jacob, Mat, Clabber—y'all go home. You Bing and Ding, go back to that bayou."

After looking across the room at everybody, he turned back to Clatoo standing at the other end of the firehalf.

"Do what you can with all this old junk around here," he said. "If the people want it, give it to them. If they don't, throw it away. I'm tired, like all y'all must be tired. And the law done waited long enough."

We all looked at him, but nobody moved.

Then Charlie spoke from back in the kitchen. "You don't have to go nowhere, Parrain."

We all turned. Charlie had been standing back there in the dark. Then he came to the front. He was so big, so tall, he had to duck his head to come through that middle door. He was taller than any man in that room and bigger than any man in that room, and we all had to look up to him. He had on blue denims, the shirt hanging out his pants. He had been running, and he had laid down on the ground. I could smell the sweat, the field, the swamps in his clothes.

He sat down on the bed.

"One of y'all standing round ain't doing nothing, go find the law," he said.

Lou Dimes

It was dark now. She sat on the passenger side, and I was in the other seat beside her. I had tried several times to speak to her, but she refused to answer. Mapes came out of the yard and went by the car without saying anything to us. I watched him go farther down the quarters until he had crossed the railroad tracks; then I couldn't see him anymore.

I looked at Candy sitting over in the other seat.

"Maybe you don't know it," I told her. "But after tonight there's going to be a big change in your life. That old man is free of you now. When he pulled your hands off his arm and went into that room, he was setting both of you free. Do you know what I'm saying? He doesn't need you to protect him anymore, Candy. He's an old man, and what little time he's got left he wants to live it his own way."

She just sat there all tight-lipped, staring out into the darkness.

"Before I leave here tonight, I want a yes or no to where our relationship is going. If I don't get any answer at all, I won't be coming back here anymore."

She looked at me now.

"You bastard," she said. "You bastard."

"That's possible," I said. "I wasn't there. But after to-night . . ."

She slapped me. It came without warning. I had noticed her face trembling, but I hadn't expected her to hit me. I raised my hand quickly, but I stopped it in midair. And instead of hitting her back, I rubbed the side of my face.

"Thank you, Ma'am," I told her. "But I will stick around until Mapes takes him into Bayonne. That's all I'll need to end my story."

Just about then one of the old men from inside the house came out onto the porch and asked for the sheriff. I heard Aunt Glo saying that the sheriff had gone down the quarters. The old man was standing in the light from inside the room. The light threw his shadow across the porch and out into the yard. Everyone else was in darkness.

"Y'all still have a couple more minutes," I heard Griffin saying. "In case y'all wanta sing, or pray, or something."

"We're ready now," the old man said. It was Gable. I could tell by his quiet, even voice.

"Well, you go'n have to wait awhile," Griffin said. "Don't worry. He won't keep you waiting long."

Gable came down the steps. He had his gun with him.

"Where you think you going?" Griffin asked him.

Gable didn't answer him. He came out to the car where Candy and I were sitting.

"Y'all seen which way the sheriff went?" he asked.

"Down there," I said, nodding toward the field. "Wait, I'll get him for you."

While I blinked the lights a couple of times, Candy tried to get some information from Gable about what had gone on inside the house. He shook his head and told her that he was supposed to talk only to the sheriff. After blinking the lights again, I saw Mapes walking back. Gable went toward him, and they stood a moment talking, then came back together.

"Come on inside," Mapes said to me. "You might as well come along, too," he said to Candy. "Seems like you did all that work for nothing."

"What happened?" I asked, getting out of the car.

"Let her tell you," Mapes said, jerking his head toward Candy.

"I did it," Candy said. She had gotten out on the other side. "I'll swear to it in court."

"And Charlie?" Mapes asked her.

"Charlie?" I said. "Big Charlie?"

"That's right," Mapes said. "Big Charlie."

We went into the yard. Mapes told the women and children they could come inside, too. He went into the room first, then Candy, then me, and the rest followed. The place was stuffy and crowded. Everything about the place said the occupant was an old man, without a woman.

Charlie was sitting on the bed when we came in. Even sitting down, he was nearly as tall as some of the old men standing around him. After we came in, he stood up and pressed his shirttail inside his pants. He was about six seven, he weighed around two hundred and seventy-five pounds, he was jet black, with a round cannonball head and his hair cut to the skin; the whites of his eyes were too brown, his lips looked like pieces of liver. His arms bulged inside the sleeves of his denim shirt, and his torso was as round as a barrel. He and Mapes weighed about the same, but Mapes had twice as much belly. He was the quintessence of what you would picture as the super, big buck nigger.

"I'm a man, Sheriff," he said. "I'm a man."

"All right," Mapes said. "I believe you. Now, I want some of you folks to go back into the kitchen or out on the porch so we can have some room in here."

The people would not move until Mapes started calling their names individually. When they did step back, it was only a couple of inches, and soon they were pressing in closer again.

"Say, sport," Mapes said to Snookum. "How about some more of that ice water?"

"Don't start till I get back, hear, Charlie?" Snookum said.

"I'm a man, Sheriff," Charlie said. "I want the world to know I'm a man. I'm a man, Miss Candy. I'm a man, Mr. Lou. I want you to write in your paper I'm a man."

"I'll write it, Charlie," I said, looking up at him. He was three or four inches taller than I, and outweighed me, I'm sure, by at least a hundred pounds.

"I'm a man," he said. "I want the world to know it. I ain't Big Charlie, nigger boy, no more, I'm a man. Y'all hear me? A man come back. Not no nigger boy. A nigger boy run and run and run. But a man come back. I'm a man."

Snookum brought the water jug and a glass. Mapes drank two glasses of water and handed the glass back.

"Thanks, sport," he said.

"Hand it here," Charlie told Snookum.

He took the jug and raised it to his mouth, and he didn't bring it down until it was empty. He handed Snookum the empty jug.

"I'm a man, Sheriff," he said. "That's why I come back. I'm a man. Parrain. I'm a man, Parrain."

Mathu, standing in the corner by the fireplace, nodded his white head.

"You want to tell us about it, Charlie?" Mapes asked him.

"I'll tell you about it, Sheriff," Charlie said. He started, then stopped, because something else had suddenly popped in his mind. "Sheriff, I'm a man," he said to Mapes. "And just like I call you Sheriff, I think I ought to have a handle, too—like Mister. Mr. Biggs."

"Sure," Mapes said, nodding. "At this point, anything you say . . . Mr. Biggs. That goes for the rest of y'all around here,"

Mapes said to us. He was serious, too; he wasn't winking. He looked back at Charlie. "What about Candy?"

"I call her Miss Candy," Charlie said. "She can say Mr. Biggs, too."

Mapes looked back at Candy, who was standing next to Mathu. When she first came into the room, she hesitated a moment to search for him; then she pushed her way through the crowd to where he stood by the fireplace. I was too far away to hear her question, if she asked one at all; and I did not hear Mathu's answer, if he gave one. I saw only a slight nod of his head.

"Well?" Mapes said to Candy.

She nodded. I don't think she really understood why Mapes had spoken to her. But that did not matter. What did matter was that Mathu was free. She did not care about anything else.

Mapes turned back to Charlie.

"Tell me about it, Mr. Biggs," he said. "Start from the beginning, back there in the field."

"It didn't start back there in the field, Sheriff," Charlie said. "It started fifty years ago. No, not fifty; more like forty-four, forty-five years ago. 'Cause that was about the first time I run from somebody. I'm fifty now, and I'm sure I musta run when I was no more than five, 'cause I know Parrain was beating me for running when I was six. 'Cause I can remember the first time he beat me for running. You remember the first time you beat me for running, Parrain? That time Ed-de took my 'tato on my way to school?"

Mathu was looking at him as though he was not absolutely sure he was seeing him there. He nodded his head.

"All my life, all my life," Charlie said. Not to Mapes, not to us, but to himself. "That's all I ever done, all my life, was run from people. From black, from white; from nigger, from Cajun, both. All my life. Made me do what they wanted me to do, and 'bused me if I did it right, and 'bused me if I did it wrong—all my life. And I took it. I'm fifty now. Fifty years of 'busing. All my natural-born black life I took the 'busing and never hit back. You tried to make me a man, didn't you, Parrain? Didn't you?"

Mathu nodded his head again.

"It didn't do no good," Charlie said. "It took fifty years. Half a hundred—and I said I been 'bused enough. He used to 'buse me. No matter if I did twice the work any other man could do, he 'bused me anyhow. I can pick up more than any man I ever met. Give me a good plate of food, and I can work longer than any man I ever met. Pull a saw, swing a axe, stretch wire, cut ditch bank, dig postholes better than any man I ever met. Still he 'bused me. Cussed me for no cause at all. Nigger this, nigger that, for no cause at all. Just to 'buse me. And long as I was Big Charlie, nigger boy, I took it."

His voice had been mounting. He had been moving about the room, the people pressing back against one another as he came toward them. He took a quarter of the space with him whether he went toward the door, or the window. He was black as tar, his round head and face sweating. I saw his round black sweaty face twitching, then trembling, and he stopped pacing the floor and raised those two big tree limbs up over his head, and, like some overcome preacher behind the pulpit, he cried out: "But they comes a day! They comes a day when a man must be a man. They comes a day!" The two big tree limbs with the big fists like cannonballs shook toward the ceiling, and we watched in awe, in fear, in case he decided to whirl around, or fall. He did neither. He brought his arms down slowly, breathing heavily, while he stared over our heads toward the wall. "They comes a day," he said to himself, not to us. "They comes a day."

"And, Mr. Biggs?" Mapes said after a respectful moment of silence.

Charlie looked at him as if he were coming out of a trance. "You said something, Sheriff?"

"What happened out there in the field between you and Beau?" Mapes asked him.

"He cussed me," Charlie said to Mapes. "I was doing my work good. Cussed me anyhow. I told him he didn't need to cuss me like that. I told him I was doing my work good. He told me he wouldn't just cuss me, but he would beat me, too. I told him no, I wasn't go'n 'low that no more, 'cause I was fifty years old—half a hundred. He told me if I said one more word, he was go'n show me how he treated a half-a-hundred-year-old nigger." Charlie stopped and looked at Mapes, shaking his head. Beads of sweat popped out of his skull, running in lines down the sides of his face. "You don't talk to a man like that, Sheriff, not when he reach half a hundred."

Mapes nodded, agreeing with him. Mapes told the people to give Charlie air. The people moved back an inch, but closed in again.

"Go on," Mapes said. "Then what?"

"I told him I was quitting," Charlie said. "I jumped down from the loader. I was coming home. He got down off that tractor and came at me with a stalka cane. I grabbed me one, too. I don't know why I did it. I had never done nothing like that in my life before. But I did it today. Bent over and got me a stalka cane just like he had. That made him stop for a second, then he started grinning at me. Grinning, just grinning at me. He knowed I wasn't go'n hit him. That's what he thought. And he came on me. He caught me twice, once on the shoulder, once in the side. Then I swung back. I caught him side the head, and down he went. I saw his head bleeding, and I thought I had kilt him, and I started running for the quarters. I came here and told Parrain what I had done. While we was standing there talking, I heard the tractor coming up the quarters, and I knowed then I hadn't kilt him.

But I told Parrain I was go'n run anyhow, 'cause he was go'n beat me now for sure if he caught me. Parrain told me if I run from Beau Boutan he was go'n beat me himself. He told me he was eighty-two, but he was more man than me, and if I run from Beau he was go'n beat me himself." Charlie looked at Mathu. Mathu nodded. But he wasn't sure that it was Charlie doing this talking. The rest of the people seemed to feel the same way. Charlie? Charlie fight back? I felt that way, too. But then I hadn't expected to see all of them here, either. "He stopped that tractor out there and jumped down with that shotgun," Charlie said to Mapes. "He kept that shotgun with him all the time, on that tractor, or in that pickup truck. He kept it all the time. Parrain told me he had a gun there, too, and he said he rather see me laying there dead than to run from another man when I was fifty years old. Beau was coming in the yard, putting a shell in the gun. Parrain reached and got his gun and pushed it in my hand. I didn't want take the gun, but I could tell in Parrain's face if I didn't, he was go'n stop Beau himself, and then he was go'n stop me, too. I took the gun and swung round, and I told Beau to stop. I told him more than once to stop. He kept on coming toward the garry. He knowed I had never done nothing like that, never even thought about doing nothing like that. But they comes a day, Sheriff, they comes a day when a man got to stand. I don't know how I did it. But I helt that gun steady as a rock. Not a tremble, not a move, steady as a rock. He kept coming toward the garry. Just grinning and grinning. Said: 'Nigger, I was go'n have a little fun with you first. Was go'n hunt you like a rabbit, and shoot you when I got tired. But now look like I ain't go'n waste my time.' He raised his gun, and I pulled the trigger."

Charlie stopped and lowered his head. We were all stunned, all remained quiet. You could have heard hearts beat in that stuffy room.

"What happened after that?" Mapes asked him after a respectful amount of time.

Charlie raised his head to look at Mapes. He was tired. The whites of his eyes had turned reddish brown. He took in a couple of deep breaths and started talking again.

"I told Parrain I was scared. I told him I was go'n run and try to reach the North. I told him they was bound to put me in the 'lectric chair now. I told him he had to say he did it, 'cause they didn't put people old as him in the 'lectric chair. I told him he was go'n die soon, and he could die in jail soon as he could die in this old house. I told him he was my parrain, and he ought to take the blame for me. I told him Candy would protect him no matter what. And while I was there begging him, I seen the dust coming down the quarters. When I seen it was Candy, I handed Parrain the gun, and I ducked back through the house. I heard Candy screaming. I was laying back there in the weeds in the back yard. I heard her asking Parrain what in the world he had done. I didn't hear Parrain answer her. I laid there flat on the ground, praying, praying he didn't say my name. I heard Candy begging him to please tell her what had happened. He didn't say a word—I didn't hear him say a word—and I got up and started running. I ran, I ran, I ran—I don't know how long. But no matter where I went, where I turnt, I was still on Marshall place. If I went toward Pichot, before I got there, something stopped me. If I turnt and went toward Morgan, something stopped me. If I went toward that highway on the back, something there stopped me, too. Something like a wall, a wall I couldn't see, but it stopped me every time. I fell on the ground and screamed and screamed. I bit in the ground. I got a handful of dirt and stuffed in my mouth, trying to kill myself. Then I just laid there, laid there, laid there. Sometime round sundown—no, just 'fore sundown, I heard a voice calling my name. I laid there listening, listening, listening, but I didn't hear it no more. But I knowed that voice was calling me back here."

He was breathing heavily, his closely shaven head was covered with beads of sweat. He was exhausted. But there was something in his face that you see in faces of people who have just found religion. It was a look of having been freed of this world. He passed his hand over his sweaty face and head; then he looked at Mathu.

"All right, Parrain?"

Mathu nodded his head. He was proud of Charlie. But the rest of us were stunned. I was still trying to figure out if any of this was happening, or had happened.

"I'm ready to go, Sheriff," Charlie said to Mapes. "I'm ready to pay. I done dropped a heavy load. Now I know I'm a man."

"After you, Mr. Biggs," Mapes said, and nodded toward the door.

"What's that you called me, Sheriff?" Charlie asked him.

"Mr. Biggs," Mapes said, and with sincerity.

Charlie grinned—a great, big, wide-mouth, big-teeth grin. It was a deep, all-heart, true grin, a grin from a man who had been a boy fifty years.

"Y'all heard that?" he said to the people around him. "Y'all heard that? Mr. Biggs. Y'all heard him, huh? Now y'all go on home. For a bunch of old men, y'all did all right today. Now go on home. Let a man through."

He led the way, with Mapes following.

But they had no sooner stepped out onto the porch when a voice in the dark called out: "Hand him over, Mapes."

That voice was Luke Will's.

Sidney Brooks

aka

Coot

———

We was go'n walk him to the car, we was go'n all shake his hand, we was go'n watch the car leave, and then we was go'n all go home.

But Luke Will had to show up.

Charlie was in front leading the way. Mapes was right behind him. Then Mathu, then Candy, Lou, Clatoo, and me. When Luke Will called out there in the road, nobody but Charlie and Mapes had gone through the door. Mapes blocked the door to keep the rest of us inside, and he hollered for Charlie to hit the floor.

Charlie said: "Me hit the floor? Hit the floor for what, for something like Luke Will? I ain't scared of no Luke Will, man."

He pushed Mapes out his way and came on back inside. He went up to Mathu and reached out his hand.

"I'm go'n need it again, Parrain."

Mathu pushed it on him, and grinned. He was proud of Charlie. Charlie swung back toward the door with the gun ready.

"Let me handle this," Mapes said.

"This my fight," Charlie said. "He come here to lynch me, not you."

"This everybody's fight," Clatoo said. "It ain't go'n be no lynching here tonight."

"Y'all stay back inside," Mapes said. "What you go'n do with them empty shotguns, use them for clubs?"

"They was empty," Clatoo said. "If you think they still empty, turn your head."

Mapes was standing in the door, filling the door. He looked back.

Clatoo had broke down the barrel. The rest of us was all doing the same.

"That's right," Clatoo said. "Every man in here got a loaded gun, and extras in his pocket. We wasn't scrapping pecans backa that house."

"You'll pay for this," Mapes said to Clatoo.

"No, he go'n pay for it out there," Clatoo said, nodding outside. "He go'n pay for a lot of things."

Mapes looked at Clatoo; then he looked at the rest of us. Nobody looked down, so he turned back and called to Luke Will.

"Go home, Luke Will," he said.

"You send that nigger out here and I'll go home," Luke Will called back.

"You got your answer, Sheriff," Charlie said. "Now you go'n move?"

Mapes glanced back over his shoulder and started calling to his deputy. He was calling, not loud, just out the left corner of his mouth. That little deputy was in the back of the room. He had his gun out, holding it, looking at it, but he wasn't moving toward Mapes. Mapes called him again.

"I ain't raising my hand against no white folks for no niggers," Griffin answered him.

"Well, Sheriff?" Charlie said.

Mapes didn't look at Charlie or answer Charlie. He looked back toward the road.

"Luke Will, what happened to Hilly?" he called.

"I put him to sleep for a while, he's all right," Luke Will called back. "You sending that nigger out here or not?"

Mapes started 'cross the garry.

"Don't act no fool, Mapes," Luke Will called. "I can see every step you make. Don't act no fool, now."

Mapes had left his gun propped against the steps, and I saw him looking over there as he crossed the garry.

Luke Will hollered at him again. "Don't come out here by yourself, Mapes. I'm warning you, now."

Mapes snatched the gun from against the steps as he hit the ground. I was standing in the door between Charlie and Clatoo, and I could see Mapes good. I saw him knock off the safety and swing the gun to the crook of his other arm. Before he could make two more steps, you had a shot and Mapes went down. They hadn't killed him, just winged him, 'cause I could see him grabbing his arm, trying to get back up. He was too big to get up.

When that gun went off, Charlie and Clatoo bust out the door, and I wasn't too far behind them. Charlie went right, toward down the quarters. Clatoo went left, into Mathu's garden, but he didn't stop there. He kept going through the garden, over into the weeds, and I wasn't more than a step behind him.

I could hear screaming back there in the house. I could hear shooting in the house, and even more screaming. Somebody opened the window, 'cause the light from the window fell across the garden, and me and Clatoo hit the ground and started crawling through the weeds. The weeds was dry, and you could hear it breaking, and the people in the road started shooting at us, but we kept down. When we reached that barbed-wire fence next to Rufe's old house, we laid down and kept quiet. I could hear Clatoo breathing hard, and I was just as tired. I had scratched my face in two or three places crawling through the weeds.

I could still hear lot of shooting from the house. Not everybody had got out, 'cause every now and then you could see a shadow go by the window. Every time a shadow went by the window, somebody from the road shot back at the house.

"I want to get that son of a bitch myself," Clatoo said.

"No more than I do," I said. "We didn't all get a chance at Beau, but we got a chance at him."

We crawled closer to the ditch so we could get a better look at the tractor. But it was so dark, and the weeds so thick, you couldn't see a thing till somebody shot. Then all you could see was the red fire from the gun.

I could hear the weeds cracking behind us, and I looked back, and I saw Mat, Jacob, and the Lejeune brothers crawling over to us.

"Everybody all right?" Clatoo asked.

"I think so," Mat said. "Little scratches here and there, but all right."

"Who was doing all that shooting in the house?" Clatoo asked.

Jacob laughed. "Billy Washington and Jean Pierre. That's why I thought it was safer out here."

"Nobody got hurt?" Clatoo asked.

"Just the ceiling," Jacob said.

"Thank God," Clatoo said.

We laid there quiet for a while.

"What now?" Mat said. He was right up against me, and he was breathing hard.

"We got to spread out," Clatoo said. He turned on his side and looked back at us. "Mat, you and Jacob get in Rufe's yard by that mulberry tree. Bing, you and Ding go farther up the quarters and cross the road. Holler, and fire. Mat, you and Jacob fire next, then me and Coot, and I just hope the rest of 'em do the same."

Mat and Jacob started out first, then Bing and Ding Lejeune. You could hear the weeds breaking as they crawled over into Rufe's yard. And even after the Lejeunes had gone all the way up to Corrine's house, you could still hear dry weeds breaking. Them over by the tractor shot each time they heard the weeds breaking.

Me and Clatoo lay there waiting for the two Lejeunes to cross the road, and I could hear Jameson over by the house calling on God to have mercy on all of us. If it wasn't Jameson calling on God, it was Glo calling for her little grandson Snookum. Jameson, then Glo; Glo, then Jameson. I heard Dirty Red call to Rooster to go shoot Jameson and shut him up. Jameson musta heard it too. There wasn't another word from him.

The Lejeunes had crossed the road. Now one hooted, and both of them fired. Them at the tractor fired back in that direction. Mat and Jacob hooted, and fired. The ones at the tractor turned and fired that way. Clatoo looked at me and nodded. We both got on our knees, hooted, fired, and fell back down. We got one of them, 'cause I could hear his scream. Me and Clatoo looked at each other and grinned, and reloaded.

From down the quarters, everybody was firing. I could tell Rooster's high-pitched voice, Dirty Red's dry, hoarse voice— and Yank's voice. Yank didn't hoot like the rest of us. He hollered the way you holler at a rodeo when somebody's riding a bucking horse. "Ya-hoo," and shot. They had spread out good, and now all the way down the quarters they was hooting and shooting. I didn't know the last time I had felt so good. Not since I was a young man in the war. Lord, have mercy, Jesus.

"You got anything left?" Clatoo asked me.

"Two more," I said.

"We'll shoot again, and save the last one," Clatoo said.

He got up on his knees and elbow and cupped his mouth to throw his voice.

"Mat, Jacob, Ding, Bing, fire at that tractor."

They hooted and fired. You woulda thought you was listening to a bunch of Indians—Lord, have mercy. Clatoo looked at me. We got up quick, fired, and fell back down. Clatoo turned on his side and cupped his mouth: "Down the quarters—fire." And down the quarters, they was firing even before Clatoo had finished saying it.

Snookum

They was shooting everywhere. Soon as the sheriff went down, they started shooting. Shooting out the front door, shooting out the window, shooting up in the ceiling—shooting everywhere. Just hollering and shooting. I told myself, boy, you better get out of here. Gram Mon had Toddy and Minnie by the hands and hollered for me to stop, but I told myself, no indeed, I'm getting out of here while the getting is good, and I shot out through the kitchen and went under the house. Then I started crawling toward the front. I didn't stop till I had reached the front steps.

Now I could see the sheriff, old Mapes, sitting out there on the walk, trying to get up. Rocking this way, that way like one of them big old scoiling kettles—trying his best to get up. But he was too big to make it by himself, and I sure wasn't going out there to help him.

The people was still shooting and hollering. I could hear them in the house over my head, shooting and hollering. I could hear Gram Mon calling me; Reverend Jameson calling the Lord—the rest of them just shooting and hollering.

Then I saw Lou crawling fast on the other side of the house. He was crawling on his knees and his elbows, crawling fast. Then something made him stop, and he looked under the house at me. It was dark under there, and it took him a good while to make me out.

"Snookum, that's you under there?"

"Yes, sir."

"Don't you hear your gram mon?"

"Yes, sir."

"Get to the back," he said.

I didn't answer him. I wasn't going back there either. Gram Mon wasn't going to beat me for not answering her the first time.

"Stay down," Lou said, and started crawling again. He was carrying a pistol. He crawled over to where Mapes was sitting on the walk rocking, rocking, trying to get up. "You all right?" he asked him.

"Sure," Mapes said. "I'm just sitting here for the view."

"Your deputy resigned," Lou said, showing Mapes the pistol.

"Keep it," Mapes said. "Anybody else got hurt?"

"I don't think so."

Mapes tried to get up again, but he was too big.

"You need help?" Lou asked him.

"More than you can give," Mapes said. "You're in charge. Raise your right hand. You do swear—"

"Like hell," Lou said.

"You're still in charge," Mapes said. "Now, don't bother me anymore tonight."

"What am I supposed to do?" Lou asked him.

"You figure that out," Mapes said. "Just leave me alone."

Horace Thompson

aka

Sharp
———

Leroy got winged. It wasn't bad, no more than a scratch, but he was over there sniveling like a gut-hanging dog. Luke told him to shut up, we all told him to shut up, but he went on sniveling, sniveling like some kinda gut-hanging dog.

"I'm dying," he said. "I'm dying. Y'all don't even care."

"If you don't shut up, you will be dying," Henry told him. "Big killer you turned out to be."

"Y'all didn't say they had all them guns," he said.

"No shit," Henry said.

"I'm dying," he said.

"Shut him up," Luke whispered. "Shut him up."

"Shut up," Henry whispered viciously. Then I heard a slap. "Shut the fuck up."

Now he really started his sniveling.

"I'm go'n give myself up, I'm go'n give myself up."

"You walk out of here, and I'll blow your back off," Henry said. "You in it, fucker. You go'n stay here till the end."

"Mapes?" Leroy called. "Mapes?"

"Shut up," Henry said, and hit him in the mouth.

"No," he said, crying. "Mapes?" he called.

"What?" Mapes answered from the yard. We couldn't see him, only hear him. From his voice, he sounded weak. Luke hadn't intended to kill him when he shot him, only to stop him. "What you want?" he called back.

"This here is Leroy. Leroy Hall. I ain't nothing but a child, Mapes."

"That's too bad," Mapes called back.

"I'm a white boy, Mapes," Leroy called.

"That's too bad, too," Mapes said.

"Satisfied now, fucker?" Henry said.

He got crazy with his sniveling now. He was all bent over with his sniveling. Just coughing and spitting. If the niggers didn't know where we were before, they sure knew where we were now.

Luke inched a little bit from behind the back tire of the tractor out into the road. He looked up the quarters, down the quarters, then moved back.

"Seen anything?" I asked him.

"How can you see a nigger at night?" he said to me. "Hey, Mapes?" he called.

"What you want, Luke Will?" Mapes called back.

"Got a boy hurt pretty bad. I want to get him outa here."

"Go on and take him out," Mapes said.

"Them niggers will shoot us."

"Shoot them back," Mapes said. "Shoot them like you shot me."

"One of them niggers shot you. We didn't shoot you."

"I have witnesses you did it," Mapes called. He rested a second before he went on. "And you're going to pay for it. Every last one of you." He rested again. "If you get out of here alive."

"He want them niggers to kill us." Leroy started sniveling again. "He want them niggers to kill us."

"And I told you to shut up," Luke said, and swung around and kicked him. He kicked him again and again. "I told you to shut up, to shut up, to shut up," he said, kicking him.

Henry, Alcee, and I grabbed Luke and held him down while Leroy crawled out of the way.

"Take it easy, Luke," I said. I had him by the shoulders. "Take it easy, Luke. Take it easy."

He was breathing hard. He had tired himself out kicking Leroy. But he had enough strength to raise his arm and knock the hell out of me. Any other time he woulda had a fight on his hands, but I knew what was bothering him now. He had brought us here, and now everything had backfired, and he didn't know how to get out of it.

Leroy was laying over there in the ditch, balled up on his elbows and knees. Nobody paid him any mind.

Luke moved up against the tire again.

"Mapes," he called. "I'm out of bullets. You go'n let them niggers shoot us down like dogs?"

Mapes didn't answer him. But Charlie did, from down the quarters. You could hear him, but you couldn't see the black ape.

"I got some extra shells," he called to Luke. "How many you need, Luke Will? Send one of your boys to come get 'em."

"I wonder what them niggers been drinking to make them all so brave," I said to Luke.

Luke moved around the tire and looked down the quarters; then he moved back against the tire again.

"They all over the place, Luke," I said. "Ain't no way we can get out of this."

"You backing out too?" he asked.

"No," I said.

I knew him too well. He could be mean when he wanted to. Mean toward anybody. He looked at me a while; then he looked at Alcee and Henry under the front trailer.

"Y'all boys all had enough, huh?" he asked. "Is that it?"

We had enough, but nobody would dare say it.

"I hope y'all know how Clyde's going to take this," Luke said, and moved back against the tire. "Say, Mapes?" he called toward the house. "Call them niggers off, we ready to turn ourselfs in."

Mapes didn't answer him.

"Mapes, can you hear me?" Luke called again.

"I can hear you," Mapes said. He sounded weaker than he did before. "Talk to Dimes. He's in charge."

"Hey, Dimes," Luke called.

"I can hear you, Luke Will," Dimes called back. Then a second later we heard him say, "Hey, Charlie—Mr. Biggs."

"That's all right, you can call me Charlie," Charlie answered from down the quarters. "We all in the dirt now, and it ain't no more Mister and no more Miss. And it ain't no deal. They go'n put me in that 'lectric chair for one, might's well put me in there for two. No deal."

"That nigger sounds like he means it," I told Luke.

Behind us, in the ditch, Leroy went on with his sniveling. Henry and Alcee lying under the front trailer looked over at Luke, waiting to hear what he had in mind. Luke looked back at them; then he looked at me—a look I had never seen before. Luke was bigger and stronger than anybody around him, never had to back down to anything. But now he looked worried, real worried.

"If you make it and I don't, look after Verna and the kids," he said to me.

"What?" I said. Because I didn't expect to hear that.

"How many shells you got left?" he asked.

"Couple," I said. "We can make a run for it. Make Tee Jack swear we never left there tonight."

"What about him?" Luke said, nodding toward Leroy.

"Fuck him," I said. "Nobody told him to get shot."

I could hear him sniveling behind me.

"Give me your shells," Luke said.

"Then I won't have any."

"Take his. He can't use them."

I passed him the two shells I had, and he put them into the gun.

"Luke," I said. "We can still get out of this. Don't do nothing foolish."

"Verna and the kids, if I don't make it," he said.

"Mapes won't let them niggers shoot us down like dogs."

He grinned to himself. Then he looked at me a long time, shaking his head.

"Mapes ain't in charge no more, Sharp," he said. "Charlie is. We got to deal with Charlie now. You ready to deal with Charlie, Sharp?"

I wasn't ready to deal with any Charlie, and he knew it. He moved back against the tire and looked down the quarters where Charlie was waiting.

Antoine Christophe

aka

Dirty Red

Charlie was up in the ditch, I was right behind him. Yank and Tucker and Chimley was over to the right. I think Clabber was somewhere back there, too. I crawled up even with Charlie and laid there 'side him. He was like a big bear laying there.

"Light me a stub, Dirty," he said.

I had a couple in my pocket, and I got out one and lit it. I handed it to him, and he took couple of good draws and handed it back to me.

"Charlie?" Lou called, from Mathu's yard.

"What you want?" Charlie answered.

"Let them turn themselves in, Charlie."

"No, sir," Charlie called back.

"It'll be murder now, Charlie," Lou said.

"It was murder before," Charlie said.

"No, Charlie," Lou called. "With Beau it was self-defense. Candy will swear to that."

Charlie didn't answer him. He reached for the cigarette, and I handed it to him. He turned his head to draw on it, so the people up the quarters couldn't see the light.

"Charlie," Lou called again.

"I ain't gone nowhere," Charlie answered him.

"I got your parrain here, Charlie," Lou said. "He wants to come out there and talk to you."

"I don't want Parrain out here," Charlie said. "Parrain told me to stand. I'm standing up to Luke Will."

It was quiet after that. Pitch black and quiet. Charlie laid there like a big old bear. And I was right there 'side him.

"You scared, Dirty?" he asked me.

"Not here 'side you, Charlie."

"Don't never be scared no more, Dirty," he told me. "Life's so sweet when you know you ain't no more coward."

I nodded my head. But I wanted some more.

"Charlie," I said.

He was looking up the quarters toward the tractor.

"Charlie," I said again.

"Yeah, Dirty?" he said, still looking up the quarters.

"What you seen back there, Charlie?"

He didn't answer me. Just laying there like a big bear, with that double-barrel shotgun 'cross his arm.

"Charlie, what you seen in them swamps?" I asked him again.

"You seen it, too, Dirty," he said, not looking at me.

"I didn't see nothing, Charlie. What did you see?" I asked him.

"All of y'all seen it," he said.

"No, I didn't see nothing," I said. "I'm just here, Charlie. Like all the rest. I didn't see nothing."

He looked back at me. "You got it, Dirty," he said. "You already got it, partner."

"Got what, Charlie?"

He grinned at me. "Light me another stub, Dirty."

I fished in my pocket for another one and took it out. While I was lighting it, I heard Lou calling from Mathu's yard.

"I'm coming out there, Charlie," he said.

"You not getting my gun," Charlie called back. "Go take Luke Will's gun."

"Luke Will, I'm coming out there," Lou called.

"You ain't taking this gun," Luke Will called back to him.

It was quiet a little while. Charlie was smoking the cigarette, smoking it hard, like he had to hurry up and finish with it. Then I saw him getting up. I whispered to him to get back down, but he kept on getting up. I heard Lou hollering to him to stay down, but Charlie wasn't listening to anybody. He was headed straight toward that tractor. And he hadn't made more than two, three, maybe four steps when I heard the first shot. I saw him staggering but he didn't go down; I saw him shooting but not sighting. I saw Lou out there waving his hands, telling everybody to stop, stop, stop. He was running all over the place, saying stop, stop, stop. I saw Charlie still going toward that tractor, but he wasn't shooting now, just falling, slowly, slowly, slowly till he had hit the ground. Then you had nothing but shooting from then on. I was shooting, and it sounded like everybody in the world was shooting. It went on like that for about a minute. Then it was quiet, quieter than you ever heard in your life.

Then we all gathered out in the road. Over by the tractor, I saw Lou standing over somebody laying back against one of the tractor wheels. I heard somebody saying that we had got the son of a bitch.

But we had all gathered around Charlie. Mathu had knelt down 'side him and raised his head out of the dust. They had really got him. Right in the belly. He laid there like a big old bear looking up at us. He was trying to say something, but it never came out. He kept on looking at us, but after a while you could tell he wasn't seeing us no more. I leaned over and touched him, hoping that some of that stuff he had found back there in the swamps might rub off on me. After I touched him, the rest of the men did the same. Then the women, even Candy. Then Glo told her grandchildren they must touch him, too.

Lou Dimes

There were three funerals two days later. Beau and Luke Will were buried in Bayonne; Charlie was buried at Marshall. The trial took place the following week, lasting three days. Candy hired her own lawyer, Clinton, to defend the blacks. The Klans defended Luke Will's friends. And you've never seen a sadder bunch of killers in all your life—on either side. Everybody had something wrong with him—scratches, bruises, cuts, gashes. They had cut themselves on barbed wire, tin cans, broken bottles—you name it. Some had sprained their ankles jumping over ditches; others had sprained their wrists falling down on the ground. And some had just run into each other. Everybody was either limping, his arm in a sling, or there was a bandage round his head or some other part of his body. Out of all that, only one had been shot—Leroy.

They had all taken baths, and wore their best clothes. For three days, if you sat close enough to the front, you smelled nothing but Lifebuoy soap and mothballs.

The courthouse was packed every day, about an equal number of blacks and whites, with nearly half being people from the news media. They had come from all over the South. Even the national press was represented. Fix was there with his crowd—including Gil, who sat with the family. (By the way LSU beat Ole Miss, twenty-one to thirteen. Both Gil and Cal had over a hundred yards each.) The Klans and the Nazi Party were there to lend moral support to Luke Will's friends. The NAACP was there, some black militants were there, and so were the state troopers, who stood by watching all and searching most of those who went in. Judge Ford Reynolds presided. Judge Reynolds is seventy, hair white as snow, face perpetually red from drinking, and he looks like the arche-typical grandfather, or what you would want your grandfather to look like. He is very rich, always happy, vain about his good looks, and has a great sense of humor. And he admitted from the beginning that not only had he never presided over a case quite like this one, but that he had never heard of one like this in all his thirty-five years on the bench. He warned that the trial would be conducted orderly. And he further warned the court that they should not mistake that old white-headed man on the bench as soft, because he could be as hard as anyone else, and harder if need be.

"All right," he said. "Swear in your first witness. Let's get started."

As I said, the trial went on for three days, and it was orderly most of the time. But every now and then one of the old black fellows, arm in sling, or forehead bandaged, knowing he was in the public eye, would go just a little overboard de-scribing what had happened. Besides, he would use all nick-names for his compatriots—Clabber, Dirty Red, Coot, Chim-ley, Rooster. This would bring the court to laughing, especially the news people, who took the whole thing as something astonishing but not serious. No one else laughed nearly as much as the news people did; that is, until Mapes took the stand a second time to explain exactly where he was during the shooting. Before, he had told the court that he was somewhere in the yard. But now the D.A. wanted to know exactly where in the yard. Mapes refused to answer. Judge Reynolds cautioned that if he did not answer he could be charged with negligence of duty, seeing that two men had been killed. Mapes answered, but only for the D.A. to hear. The D.A. demanded that he speak loud enough so that the entire court could hear him. Mapes looked at the D.A. with those hard gray eyes, as if he were about to spring out of that chair and punch him, but instead said: "The whole fight, I was sitting on my ass in the middle of the walk. Luke Will shot me, and I was sitting on my ass in the middle of the walk. Now, is that loud enough?" And he got up from the witness chair and returned to the other seat. That's when everyone in the courtroom started laughing, including Judge Reynolds. The people passing by out on the street must have thought we were showing a Charlie Chaplin movie in there. That happened the morning of the third day, and until that evening when the trial finally ended, people were still laughing. Mapes, with his left arm in a sling, stayed red all day, and would probably stay red for years to come.

The jury deliberated three hours, then returned with the verdict. After reading it and studying it for a moment, the judge told all defendants to rise, black and white alike. He said since the two men who had killed were both dead, being the same two who had killed Beau and shot Mapes, he could not pass judgment over them, but ask that their souls rest in peace. But for the others, he said he was putting all of them on probation for the next five years, or until their deaths—whichever came first. He said that meant he was taking away their privilege of carrying any kind of firing arm, rifle, shotgun, or pistol, or being within ten feet of anyone else with such weapons. (That was like telling a Louisianian never to say Mardi Gras or Huey Long.) He said if he heard once that any of the defendants picked up a gun, or was within ten feet of anyone with such weapon, he would send that person to prison for the rest of his natural-born life. He asked if there were any questions. There were no questions, and he slammed down the gavel and said court was adjourned.

Candy and I went out of the courtroom and stood out on the steps and watched the people leave. She asked Mathu if he wanted her to take him back home. He told her no; he told her Clatoo was there in the truck, and he would go back with Clatoo and the rest of the people. The old truck was parked in front of the courthouse, and we watched them all pile in. Candy waved goodbye to them. I felt her other hand against me, searching for my hand; then I felt her squeezing my fingers.

ALSO BY
ERNEST J. GAINES

CATHERINE CARMIER

A compelling love story set in a deceptively bucolic Louisiana countryside, where blacks, Cajuns, and whites maintain an uneasy coexistence.

"[Gaines's] best writing is marked by what Ralph Ellison, describing the blues, called 'near-tragic, near-comic lyricism.'" —*Newsweek*
0-679-73891-6

IN MY FATHER'S HOUSE

In St. Adrienne, a small rural black community in Louisiana, the Reverend Phillip Martin comes face to face with the sins of his youth in the person of Robert X, a young, unkempt, vaguely sinister stranger who arrives in town for a mysterious "meeting" with the Reverend.

"A mature and muscular novel . . . [with] variety and richness."
—*The New York Times Book Review*
0-679-72791-4

A LESSON BEFORE DYING

Set in a small Cajun community in the late 1940s, *A Lesson Before Dying* tells the story of a young black man sentenced to death for a murder he did not commit, and a teacher who tries to impart to him his learning and pride before the execution.

"This majestic, moving novel is an instant classic, a book that will be read, discussed and taught beyond the rest of our lives."
—*Chicago Tribune*
Winner of the National Book Critics Circle Award for Fiction
0-679-74166-6

OF LOVE AND DUST

Of Love and Dust is a tale of a contest of wills between two men—Marcus, a prisoner sent to work in the fields, and Bonbon, his Cajun overseer.

"Gaines knows how to tell a story . . . [He writes] with humor, a strong sense of drama and a compassionate understanding of people who find themselves in opposing poitions." —*Washington Post*
0-679-75248-X

VINTAGE CONTEMPORARIES

AVAILABLE AT YOUR LOCAL BOOKSTORE, OR CALL TOLL-FREE
TO ORDER: 1-800-793-2665 (CREDIT CARDS ONLY).